"I'm accused of making love to you for a specific reason."

Francis's voice was becoming more cynical with each observation. "If we discount true love, then it must be for gain, and if it's gain, then it must be Copperthwaite. You believe that as you're your grandfather's heir, I'm after your inheritance—"

"I don't want to think that," Philippa broke in angrily, "but what other explanation is there?"

"It has, I suppose, crossed your mind that you might not be in his will?"

"Of course it has!"

"It might, I suppose, have crossed my mind, too?" Francis suggested quietly.

He seemed to be playing a game with her heart. Philippa didn't know whether to wipe the smile from his face or throw herself into his arms.

JACQUELINE GILBERT began writing for the Harlequin Presents series in 1976. She has since written approximately one romance novel a year, a pace that allows her a good deal of time to devote to her family. "In the final analysis," she says, "the family is the only stable and significant thing in our lives." She and her husband, the person she credits most for helping her to become the person she is today, live in England's Midlands and count themselves lucky to have both children and grandchildren.

Books by Jacqueline Gilbert

HARLEQUIN PRESENTS
160—DEAR VILLAIN
600—A HOUSE CALLED BELLEVIGNE
801—CAPRICORN MAN

HARLEQUIN ROMANCE
2102—EVERY WISE MAN
2214—COUNTRY COUSIN
2308—SCORPIO SUMMER
2492—THE TRODDEN PATHS
2631—THE CHEQUERED SILENCE

These books may be available at your local bookseller.

Don't miss any of our special offers. Write to us at the following address for information on our newest releases.

Harlequin Reader Service
901 Fuhrmann Blvd., P.O. Box 1397, Buffalo, NY 14240
Canadian address: P.O. Box 603,
Fort Erie, Ont. L2A 9Z9

JACQUELINE GILBERT

poppy girl

Harlequin Books

TORONTO • NEW YORK • LONDON
AMSTERDAM • PARIS • SYDNEY • HAMBURG
STOCKHOLM • ATHENS • TOKYO • MILAN

For
Pat and Peter
fellow francophiles
and adopted Cumbrians

Harlequin Presents first edition November 1986
ISBN 0-373-10929-6

Original hardcover edition published in 1986
by Mills & Boon Limited

CHAPTER ONE

ON an afternoon in early May the city of Orange, in that region of France known as Provence, was enjoying blue skies and a blazing sun. The open-air Roman theatre, always a focal point for visitors, had just re-opened after lunch and a small group of English tourists were gathered round the talking-guide machine, digging into their pockets and handbags in search of the required coins—two francs—to make the machine work.

Philippa Ingram, sitting half-way back in the auditorium, looked down on them, her attention caught by their raised voices. Elbows resting on the stone step behind her, bare legs and sandalled feet outstretched for coolness, she listened to the frustrated voices and then tried to block them out. It was a lovely day and the sun was making her feel lazy. She could feel it burning her bare arms and legs and she wafted the pages of the guide book she was reading back and forth to create a breeze.

As Philippa looked round the theatre, her interest quickening, it was easy to allow a sense of history to take over. For the huge, austere stonework backing the stage was incredibly awe-inspiring, and the size of the whole place made her feel extremely small and insignificant.

Unfortunately, history was being upstaged by her fellow-countrymen. The francs needed to work the machine, which provided a short history of the theatre available in four languages, were proving

7

elusive. Philippa's eyes returned unwillingly to the
group. Really, she thought in mild exasperation,
among six people, surely they could come up with a
couple of francs! Almost on the thought, one was
found and as the search continued Philippa
burrowed into her canvas shoulder bag, deciding
she was not going to have any peace and quiet
until the other was produced. She began to climb
down the steep steps that made up the seating
arrangements of the theatre, her coming noticed,
faces turning expectantly. One of the group, a man
wearing a bright check shirt, had already shown an
interest in Philippa's solitary state and how darted
towards her. Before he could say anything, she
held out the coin and to avoid encouragement
adopted a cool, practical manner, saying,

'I have a franc here, if it helps.'

Check shirt beamed up at her. 'That's kind of
you. Would you like to join us? It should be
interesting.'

Philippa dropped the coin into his open palm.
'Thanks, but I'm getting all I need from this,' and
she held up the guide book still in her hand. She
smiled to the group in general and made her way
back up the steps, very conscious of his eyes still
on her. Resuming her seat, she shielded her own
from the sun and peered up at the imposing statue
of the Emperor Augustus who had originally built
the theatre in 14 B.C. Holding his general's baton,
the stone figure dominated the huge interior stage
wall from his arched cavity high up, centre stage.

There must have been jubilation when the
archaeologists found him and pieced him together
again, Philippa mused, and sensitive to atmosphere, she imagined the massive auditorium filled
with ten thousand conquering Romans. Only

seven thousand spectators could be accommodated now. She grinned. *Only* seven? Dear, dear!

The acoustics were supposed to be excellent, and proof was now given as audible words of disappointment began to float upwards. The guide machine, it seemed, was out of order. Philippa groaned a laugh. She could imagine the thoughts flying through Check Shirt's head at this moment, no doubt remembering her guide book. Well, he could borrow it with pleasure, she decided with mischievous amusement, but she hoped he could read French. Assistance came from an unexpected quarter.

'Can I help?' The question, coming from below, immediately arrested Philippa's attention. It came from a man who had been studying Augustus's statue and who now walked with an easy stride to the group. His voice, pleasantly friendly, held a hint of diffidence, allowing his offer to be declined without embarrassment should it not be taken up.

No fear of that, observed Philippa with amusement, as the two women in the group fought over who should explain the faulty machine. Saved by a Good Samaritan—and rather an intriguing one. She had noticed him earlier, could not help noticing him, for he was in front of her in the queue for the entrance tickets, talking in French to his companion, an attractive brunette. Her curiosity now grew as she listened to his excellent, idiomatic English.

Languages being her own line of business, Philippa was intrigued. It was not uncommon for a Frenchman to be able to speak English, but for him to be so comfortable in the language was interesting, and he certainly knew his history. He dealt briefly with the Roman occupation and was now saying, his voice a low drawl as if he found some amusement in the role he was taking, 'Plays and concerts are held here, which is good, don't you think? A pity to waste such a magnificent setting.' He bent his head towards a questioner and nodded. 'Yes, incredible, isn't it?' and all eyes turned to the interior stage wall. 'Orange is the only Roman theatre in existence with the *frons scenae* miraculously intact.' There were murmurs of appreciation from his listeners. 'The acoustics,' and here he swung round and allowed his gaze to sweep the curved auditorium, lingering momentarily on Philippa in her solitary spot half-way up, before coming back to the group, '... are excellent. You can try them out if you're feeling energetic. About forty rows to the top, I believe, but don't forget to leave one of you down here on the stage, to say something, will you?' There was a teasing note in his voice which produced chuckles from his listeners.

Philippa closed the guide book and searched the sky. There was not a cloud in sight and the blue heavens made a magnificent ceiling to the theatre. It might not be a bad idea to take her photographs now, before the peace began to fill up, she decided, and collecting her things together, she stood up. How many steps had he said? Forty? Then she had about twenty to go. Not stopping to take a breather, she arrived at the top, panting slightly, and leaned on the back stonework, arms folded on the shoulder-high retaining wall. The scene that greeted her was one of roof-tops in reds and blues and, beyond the city, distant green hills shimmered in the heat. There was a slight breeze up here and Philippa closed her eyes and lifted her face to it.

It was a vulnerable face she turned to the sky,

one which she did not often allow the world to see. A face not at first glance any way remarkable, being rather too strong on character for some who only saw the obstinate chin, the disconcerting level stare from large brown eyes, and a mobile mouth that could pull down in an uncompromising grimace of disagreement. Only her closest friends knew of her wicked sense of humour, her loyalty to those she held dear, her refreshing honesty. Philippa Ingram had led an unconventional early life and had learned in her youth to adapt to circumstances, covering up her inner feelings. She had been the practical member of her family, the job forced upon her, and she had come to believe that that was what she was, sensible and practical. It had brought some measure of personal success and an orderly existence, but a restlessness had been growing within her of late, she could not pin its cause, and no doubt there was no single reason. Perhaps she was becoming fed up with being practical and sensible.

Two things were bothering her today. The first was the date; it was the anniversary of her father's death. The second was the envelope lying in her bag. Doubts and indecisions brought their own form of vulnerability. It had been a startling and unnerving experience to receive word from Cumbria. Her thoughts over the past weeks had been turning more and more towards her father's relations and Copperthwaite in Cumbria, his birthplace. Why she should suddenly have this curiosity about the Ingrams in England after so many years studiously ignoring them, she did not know, except it was part of the restlessness. Receiving word from them, right out of the blue, was weird.

Not a letter, but an invitation . . . to the eighty-fifth birthday celebrations of Philip Ingram, her grandfather. As if it were the most natural thing in the world for a loving granddaughter to be in attendance, when that same granddaughter and grandfather had never met. And why had they never met? Because Philip Ingram, her grandfather, had told Robert Ingram, her father, never to darken his door again, or words to that effect.

Philippa grimaced a smile, wryly amused at the dramatic turn of phrase. She came back from an imagined house called Copperthwaite stuck on some bleak fells in Cumbria and felt the sun warm on her body. She loved France, but it was here that she felt the loss of her parents the most, especially her father, for her mother, Rose, had died when she was a child. Even after seven years she missed him fiercely, missed his easy, light-hearted banter, missed organising him into some semblance of reasonable day-to-day living. If he were with her now he would be sketching, the blank page coming to life with a few swift strokes—the roof-tops, the church steeple, the pigeons perched on the nearby chimney stack . . .

'Is something the matter?'

The quiet, restrained question broke into her thoughts and Philippa stiffened, giving a quick startled glance over her shoulder before glaring balefully at the roof-tops once more. He had a light tread, this fair man. How long had he been there? Had he seen the wretched tears? She blinked furiously and said dismissively, 'No. Thank you,' showing plainly by the tone of her voice that any further comment would be unwelcome, and willing him to go, the roof-tops still blurred.

There was a slight pause. 'This, I believe, is yours.'

Damn him, why didn't he go? Philippa took a deep breath and steeled herself to turn, saying brusquely, 'What did you say?' She had an impression of tanned arms above rolled-up sleeves, piercing cornflower blue eyes and a head of corn-coloured hair.

'This franc. I'm told it's yours.' The voice was patient and controlled. The fair head nodded towards the English group now clicking cameras down below. 'They didn't want to be accused of stealing and as I was on my way up . . .' He held out a long, narrow hand and as Philippa's came up to meet it he dropped the coin carefully into her palm.

At least he had the gumption not to look at her, she thought furiously, knowing her face was bright red with embarrassment. Her anger, directed less at him and more at herself for being such a sentimental idiot, helped her to gain control.

He went on, 'They didn't need it, the franc. The machine was out of order.' He must have known the explanation was unnecessary, but she was glad of the breathing space.

He was around the six foot mark, and slim, with eyes that didn't miss much. An interesting face with a touch of arrogance in the sweep of brow, the droop of eyelid, the set of the mouth. He was, she guessed, the type to take over in an emergency and then back off. He made her feel—she struggled to analyse just what she did feel, and came up with something that gave her a jolt. This man made her aware of herself, of being a woman, and it was unnerving, for his own manner could not be criticised. He was extremely polite and the cool blue gaze was completely impersonal.

That gaze was upon her now, and thoroughly

off-balance, she glanced down at the coin in her hand and, for something to say, said, 'Hardly worth the effort of the climb.' Too late she saw the words as an invitation to a compliment and clamped her jaw with annoyance and waited for the inevitable, ready to squash him and it when it came.

She underestimated him. Lashes flickered over limpid eyes and a brow twitched, but he did not say the obvious. Instead, he observed, 'You read French,' as his eyes fell to the guide book.

'François, *viens! Nous devons partir, n'est-ce pas*?' The plaintive request to leave floated upwards. The brunette was bored and showed it.

'*J'arrive tout de suite*, Lisette,' was his answer. Lisette swept Philippa a suspicious look, shrugged an eloquent shlulder and was silent.

'I'm afraid Roman ruins do not interest my friend,' he confided with a wry smile, as if apologising for Lisette's rudeness. He had retained his French and went on, 'So if there is nothing more I can do for you . . .' His brows rose slightly, and Philippa had the feeling he would have said more under different circumstances.

'Thank you, no. It was kind of you to take the trouble.' Her own French was excellent, but she was aware that he gave no hint of surprise. Perversely, this niggled.

'In that case, I'll say goodbye,' and he gave her a nod and dropped lightly and unhurriedly down the steps.

Philippa watched them leave, the fair head bent close to the dark one. François. Francis. The name suited him—sleek, spare and silky.

She gave herself an impatient reprimand. So his name was Francis and he spoke English and

French like a native. What did it matter? She would not see him again and he would be remembered only for intruding on a stupid, silly emotional moment. She dismissed him from her mind and took up her camera, and for the next ten minutes circled the auditorium in the hope of fitting the theatre into her view-finder. When she was done she left, collecting the Metro from a side street and following the signs south to Avignon, to take tea with Sylvie.

'My dear Phippy, sightseeing in all this heat? How energetic of you!' Sylvie Rousard languidly poured the tea from an elegant Limoges pot into delicate china cups as she sat cool and composed beneath the shade of a tree. 'Was it worth it?'

'Yes, it was, as you should know.' Philippa lay on a rug on the grass, enjoying the privacy and beauty of the Rousards' walled garden. Angélique, her goddaughter, shared the rug and watched as Philippa built her a tower of coloured bricks.

Sylvie yawned daintily. 'I'm much too lazy these days to chase the ghosts of Romans.' She eyed the sprawling figure of her friend. 'Did Augustus fall off his pedestal at the sight of those legs of yours?' Sylvie was a diminutive five-two and envied her friend's extra four inches.

Philippa grinned. 'Shorts are definitely the most practical garment for climbing steep steps,' she claimed, and gave eight-month-old Angélique a succession of growling kisses on her tummy, making the baby chuckle out loud before observing, 'She's the image of Fabien, isn't she?'

'She is,' agreed her mother, 'but perhaps she will grow out of it, poor cherub. Of course, the likeness pleases my dear *Belle-mère*, which is something. She dared to voice her disappointment in Fabien's hearing that Angélique was not a boy and pouf! how she was put in her place!'

Philippa chuckled at the satisfaction in Sylvie's voice. Her mother-in-law sounded a daunting personage.

'Politely, you understand,' Sylvie went on, 'for that is Fabien's way, but she has never said it again, and secretly I believe she has come to adore the *bébé*.'

'How can she resist?' declared Philippa, allowing Angélique to pull a coloured bangle from her wrist.

'Oh, how nice it is to talk together like this!' Sylvie's dark eyes brightened. 'Remember how we talked after lights-out? And read Georgette Heyer under the covers by torchlight?'

'And cried over *Beau Geste*?'

The two friends exchanged reminiscent smiles. Sylvie pouted and heaved a sigh. 'I wish you would settle in France, Phippy.' She eyed the other girl speculatively as Philippa lay back and stared up at the sky through the branches of the tree. 'I understand why you could not return when your father died,' Sylvie went on, 'you were still studying, but Phippy, I always thought you would live in France.' There was a plaintive note in Sylvie's voice as she said this.

Philippa wrinkled up her nose thoughtfully. 'So did I, but somehow things contrived to keep me in England. The flat in Grace's house became vacant and I got my first translating job, and so I just stayed on.'

'Don't you find it constricting, living with your aunt?'

Philippa laughed and shook her head. 'I don't think of Grace as being an aunt, she's more like a

sister, or a close friend, and the house is divided
into two completely separate flats, with their own
entrance.' She cast an amused glance at her friend.
'I can have anyone I like to stay over without any
difficulty and without upsetting Grace. She's a
liberated woman and respects my privacy as I do
hers.'

'That's all very well,' retorted Sylvie with
asperity, 'but do you? Have anyone stay over, I
mean?' She scowled. 'No, no—I have no right to
ask such a question. I just want you to be happy
with the right man, Phippy!'

Philippa's eyes twinkled at Sylvie's anguished
expression. 'It's been known to happen, Sylvie, the
house guest, but not often, I have to admit—they
all seem to turn out to have feet of clay.'

'For someone who was brought up a Bohemian
and allowed to run wild for the first ten years you
are very conservative in your love life.' Sylvie's
tone was one of rueful, laughing disgust.

'That's why, Sylvie dear, that's why. I have
conflicting streaks in my character, I'm afraid, and
no illusions.'

'Have you ever fallen in love, really and truly, so
that you're no longer sensible?'

Amusement tinged Philippa's, 'No.'

Sylvie sighed deeply. 'I might have guessed! One
day, Phippy, you are going to fall in love like a . . .
like a . . .'

'Ton of bricks?'

'That will serve perfectly. A ton of bricks is
heavy enough.' Sylvie ran exasperated fingers
through her short dark curls. 'You turn those
discerning brown eyes of yours on every man you
meet and find him wanting. No man is perfect!'
and catching the raised brows of her friend she

added, laughing, 'No, not even Fabien is perfect! Somewhere there must be someone able to stab your soul with Cupid's arrow and make you lose your head, and when that happens, hooray! I shall be a most interested spectator.' She frowned. 'I cannot believe that there's been no one to stop your heart from its regular beat.' She looked encouragingly. 'No one to make your pulse race faster.'

Philippa grinned. 'Oh, there's no shortage of interesting men,' she offered, lazily biting at a piece of grass. 'The trouble is after a while they turn out to be the most complete bore. Rather deflating!'

'You might meet someone while you're here,' mused Sylvie, keeping her voice casual and gleefully brooding on one name from her guest list for that evening.

'There was the most ravishing man at the theatre this afternoon.'

Sylvie sat up. 'Really? Ravishing? Tell me more!'

'Fair, slim and aristocratic-looking,' replied Philippa dreamily, 'like a superior Afghan hound— you know the sort I mean—long and silky, looking down a slender nose rather disdainfully. Sleek and beautifully made and ready to go like the wind if let loose. Not brown eyes, but bright blue, and before you begin to get excited he was already on a leash. His owner was a brunette—sulky and very sexy.'

'What a pity,' sympathised Sylvie, dismissing the ravishing man and thinking about Jules Morin. She had been delighted to learn that he was back home and was enjoying the anticipation of introducing her best friend to one of Fabien's oldest friends, already seeing them, in her mind's eye, walking together hand in hand towards marital bliss.

During this companionable silence while Sylvie dreamed of matchmaking, Philippa was remembering Orange and the bright blue eyes, the crisp fair hair and the way his mouth curved at the corners . . .

She banished her thoughts abruptly and gave herself a mental shake. Had it come to this—mooning over a man she had met once, briefly? Changing the subject, she announced, 'I had an invitation today.'

Sylvie perked up. 'An invitation to what?'

'To my grandfather's eighty-fifth birthday. Ouch, Angel, that's my hair you're tugging, *ma petite*!' Philippa half sat up, leaning on one elbow.

Puzzled, Sylvie queried, 'Your grandfather? I thought, surely, that your grandparents were no longer living?'

Struggling with a small plump hand that had a strong hold on a fistful of hair, Philippa answered, 'You're thinking of my mother's side, the Stanhopes. No, this is my Ingram grandfather.'

'Oh, *him*—but I thought you didn't have anything to do with that side of the family?'

'I don't. He washed his hands of us all.'

'Will you go?'

'I don't know.' Philippa frowned. 'Part of me is madly curious to learn something of these relatives I've never met, and then I remember nothing came from the Ingrams when Mother died and I feel I can never forgive them for ignoring us all these years.'

'He's very wealthy, isn't he?' pondered Sylvie thoughtfully, and gave a knowing smile. 'Think of all that lovely money, Phippy!'

Philippa laughed. 'He's hardly likely to leave it to me, now is he? Dad had a sister, so there must be a few more likely candidates, and anyway, I don't want his money. I haven't even decided to go.' As she said it, Philippa suddenly realised that she would go.

Sylvie looked at her watch and gave a hurried exclamation. '*Hélas!* You must hurry or you will be late for this evening. Fabien will call for you at eight o'clock.'

'That isn't necessary,' protested Philippa. Fabien Rousard was a doctor, a paediatrician, and a busy man. 'I have my own car.'

Sylvie fluttered her hands dismissively. 'Fabien will not permit it. You must be fetched and taken home. He could not be happy otherwise.'

'Who is coming?' Philippa swung Angélique into the air, making the baby chuckle.

'Tch! Who is not coming! I thought, at first, to have a small dinner party, but the guest list has escalated so much that it is now no longer an intimate affair.' Sylvie hesitated. 'There is a friend of Fabien's I want you to meet—his name is Jules Morin, and he is very, very charming.' Before Philippa could comment she glanced at her watch again, exclaiming, 'Come, Angel, to Maman . . . Auntie Phippy must go now.' Sylvie took her daughter from Philippa and beamed a smile. 'How nice to practise my English—I so rarely get the chance, but tonight, Phippy, you can be wholly French, I promise.'

At ten minutes to eight Philippa was ready, a quick dash of perfume being all that was necessary to complete her toilette, and this she now applied. Fabien was usually prompt and she did not want to keep him waiting. She collected a silk-fringed shawl from a drawer and made for the sitting-room, hesitating at the wardrobe mirror.

She saw a young woman of medium height in a dusky pink dress of fine fabric which fitted at the waist and fell in soft folds to mid-calf. With thin straps and a low back it showed off a slim but curved figure and its simple lines suited her. Brown hair, streaked red and gold by the sun and washed barely an hour ago, was springing into slightly unmanageable waves and tamed by two strands, either side, being taken to the back and caught up with a mother-of-pearl slide. She pushed her feet into matching pink shoes and passed into the main room.

It was a pleasant flat, above a craft shop in the town of Villeneuve-lès-Avignon, which was situated on the opposite bank of the Rhône and linked to Avignon by a bridge. Fabien had found the place for her and Philippa had already lost her heart to Villeneuve, loving its narrow streets and old, quaint buildings. This house was one of a row, climbing steeply, all joined together as if for support, the front door leading directly out on to the narrow cobbled street. Opposite, the ground fell dramatically, the houses built on a lower level affording an amazing, uninterrupted view of the city of Avignon, with its crenellated walls and Popes' Palace glowing golden in the sunlight.

The view was well worth having to climb the hill. Every morning Philippa would walk down to the Place Jean Jaurés, take her place in the queue at the bakery in the square and bring back her breakfast, a warm croissant—a roll in the shape of a crescent—and bread for the day—a long stick called a *baguette*. The smell from the bakery was mouthwatering.

The door bell interrupted her thoughts and Philippa turned from the view at the window, collected clutch bag and shawl and went to answer it. She locked the door at the top of the stairs and ran down to open the outer door.

Afterwards she tried to recapture how she felt at that moment, but there were too many conflicting emotions. All she knew for certain was that colour flooded her face and with her heart pumping faster, she stammered, 'Oh! it's you . . .! I mean . . .' She took a breath and said lamely, 'Hello.'

'Hello.' He smiled, the cool, cornflower blue eyes resting thoughtfully on her face. 'You are Sylvie's friend Philippa, aren't you?' and when she nodded, still dazed by his unexpected appearance, he went on, 'It's a small world, isn't it? When Sylvie described you to me, she little realised we'd already met.' He waited a moment, giving her a chance to comment, and when she didn't, added, 'Fabien was late from hospital and so I was asked to pick you up.'

'Oh—yes, I see.' Philippa pulled herself to-gether—he must think her dim-witted!

'I'm an old friend of Fabien's. He has, perhaps, mentioned the Morins to you?'

Morin? The name rang a bell. She said, 'I think Sylvie spoke of you this afternoon as being one of her guests.'

'Ah, that would be my cousin, Jules. This afternoon Sylvie did not know I was back in town.' He pulled a droll face. 'It is always to be my fate, this confusion between me and Jules. Such an audacious fellow! When we were boys he got me into the most fearful scrapes and we became known for evermore as the terrible twins.' He had been speaking in English, taking his cue from her

startled exclamation as she opened the door, but
now he switched to French, saying gently, 'The
Roussards have a superb cook. It would be a pity
for him to hand in his notice because we are late.'
He frowned. 'You would, perhaps like to
telephone—to check I'm genuine? My name is
Francis . . .'

'Oh, no, that won't be necessary,' Philippa said
hurriedly, a wave of embarrassment sweeping over
her. Had she been staring? His presence on her
doorstep was enough to make anyone think they
were dreaming! 'Yes, of course, let's go.'

'If you will allow me?' Francis Morin pulled the
door on to its catch and putting a light impersonal
hand beneath her elbow, led her across the cobbles
to where his car was parked a few yards further
on.

CHAPTER TWO

THE car was a white Alfa Romeo Spider, sleek and powerful. Philippa waited while Francis Morin opened the passenger door and noticed that it was a right-hand drive—was he, then, English?

As she drew in her legs, the skirt of her dress caught the sill and they both reached at the same moment to tuck it in out of harm's way. Their hands touched. An insignificant thing, but Philippa pulled hers away quickly. His touch had sent a shiver through her. She told herself furiously to grow up, that she was imagining this peculiar sensitivity between herself and this man, but she knew she was fooling herself. It had never happened before, this instant attraction to a man she knew nothing about, and it was unnerving and the sooner she pulled herself together the better.

By the time Francis joined her she had regained some measure of serenity, outwardly, at least, but it was difficult to ignore him totally, good manners alone demanded that she should make some form of conversation, and the close confines of the car did not help. And if she were truthful she did not wish to ignore him, only to disguise the effect he had on her. Everything he did seemed spare of unnecessary energy. She remembered how he had lightly dropped from step to step at the theatre that afternoon, in command of his body. She thought suddenly that that seemed to sum him up. He was a man in total command of himself, and it

24

annoyed her that he had managed to ruffle her own self-possession.

A wide gold watch encircled a slim wrist, she noticed, as he reached for the ignition key. His head turned to her and those incredible blue eyes engulfed her as he asked, 'Ready?' and she nodded.

They drove past the Fort of Saint André which dominated the top of the hill and wound their way through the labyrinth of narrow streets to join the main road, traffic lights at the entrance to the Daladier Bridge halting their progress. Francis began to talk of the theatre at Orange, asking if she had been to Arles or Nîmes, and she replied, his easy, relaxed manner helping, but she was still incredibly flustered, and very much aware of him.

The casual clothes of the afternoon were gone and in their place was a cream suit, superbly cut, the jacket of which was lying across the back seat. His shirt was dark blue with a fine white stripe and was teamed with a cream silk tie. Philippa guessed the cream leather shoes were handmade Italian.

I'm not attracted to fair men, she said to herself.

The faint tang of aftershave mingled elusively with *Arpège* and body oil—it seemed that every sense was sharpened, and then she suddenly realised that Francis was waiting for her to speak. She said hurriedly, 'I'm sorry—what did you say?'

'Don't you think it's like a cut-out in a fairy book?' he repeated, indicating the view ahead. They were now travelling across the bridge, and this was exactly what the ramparts and the Palace of the Popes looked like, and Philippa murmured her agreement. Her conversation so far had hardly been impressive. Her eyes caught the four remaining arches of the St-Bénézet Bridge, stretching from the Avignon bank to mid-stream.

'I remember being so disappointed when I first saw that,' she said, and Francis, following the direction of her gaze, began to hum *Sur le Pont d'Avignon* breaking off to say,

'Probably the first bit of French that English children learn. Did you know that they couldn't have danced on the bridge? It's only wide enough to walk across and it's now thought that they danced under it, where it crossed the island in the middle of the river.' He glanced her way, smiling wryly. 'Nothing is sacred, is it? Not even a nursery rhyme.' Swinging the car round the Place Crillon, taking the road parallel to the river, he went on, 'How do you know the Rousards?'

Here was a question that needed little thought. 'I met Sylvie at school in Grenoble,' Philippa explained. 'I've only known Fabien since their marriage.'

'And what was an English girl doing at school in Grenoble?'

'My parents moved to France and settled in the south, my mother's health was not good and it was hoped that a warmer climate might suit her better.' She paused, wondering if she should go on, but he had seemed interested. 'She died when I was eight and I was sent to boarding school when I was ten.'

'Did you like it, the school?'

She laughed softly. 'I hated it at first, only Sylvie made it bearable. If it had been left to my father I wouldn't have had to go, but my mother's parents descended on us and found me running wild—at least, that's how they put it.' She laughed again, remembering. 'Oh, dear! They were good people but terribly conventional. My father was a painter and we lived a free and easy life, one in their eyes not at all ideal for a ten-year-old girl, but it suited Father and me. In the summer I virtually lived on the beach and in the sea. We rented a small house on the coast near Cap Camarat, the headland just south of St Tropez— do you know it?'

'I know St Tropez and know what the coast is like along there.'

'Our house was off the beaten track and there was a stiff climb down to the beach, which put most people off, so we were very private. Anyway, Robert, my father, didn't see anything wrong in me going with him to the local bar while he and his cronies set the world to rights, but my poor Stanhope grandparents were horrified. They were caring people and were afraid for my health because of my mother—she had lung trouble—but it was obvious I was a little toughie, so they attacked on the question of my education.' She pulled a rueful face. 'Which was unorthodox, I admit. I only went to school when I felt like it, but I could recite the histories of all the famous painters, writers and philosophers; could speak English, French, Italian and Spanish—the artist community along the coast was truly cosmopolitan so we kids were a mixed bag—and I could cook the basics, but much else was negligible. So it was either boarding school in France or back to England with them. Luckily, my father hit a good period at that time and sold a few paintings, or I could have ended up in Northamptonshire, which to me, at that time, was on another planet.' She stopped suddenly and searched his face anxiously for boredom. 'I haven't spoken about myself like this for years. What a dangerous man you are!'

He smiled slightly, his eyes turning her way briefly. 'No, no, merely a good listener. I'm interested. Tell me about your father.' She remained silent and he prompted, 'You say he was a painter?'

She nodded. 'He wasn't bothered much about anything but painting, and he didn't ask a great deal from life. He was popular, generous—he'd help anyone and spend his last franc doing it—easygoing, irresponsible and fun to be with.'

'You, I gather, kept him in order.'

Philippa chuckled. 'I tried to. He died seven years ago.' She gave a small shrug. 'He had a fall. It was a stupid thing to happen. I stayed at Grenoble until I was eighteen—I'd begun to like learning by that time and found I had an aptitude for languages. Robert decided I should get to know England and I was keen, so feelers were put out for me to finish my education there. I went to university and read languages, and during my second year, when I was twenty, Robert had this fall.'

'How old was he?'

'Forty-eight, and he was fit. Like all accidents, it shouldn't have happened. There'd been unusually heavy rain and high winds along the coast—it was February, and Robert knew the cliff path to our home well, we both did, even in the dark—you could only reach the cottage on foot from the nearest village. Anyway, he'd had a few glasses of wine with his friends, nothing in excess, they told me, but he wasn't as careful as he should have been and because of the storms the cliff had collapsed at one point and he didn't know of it, didn't see it on his walk back. He wasn't found until the next day. They sent for me, but he died before I could get there.'

Francis said gently, 'I'm sorry. It must have been an unhappy time for you.' He waited a moment and then asked, 'Was he a good painter?'

Philippa considered the question thoughtfully. 'He was good at what he did best, portraits, but there was a limited call in that line, so his bread and butter was provided by the pictures he did of the harbour at Cannes or the old back streets of Nice. You know the kind I mean, pictures the tourists take back home to remind them of a happy holiday.' She went on a little defensively, 'No good turning your nose up at the bread and butter when it can provide the cake. Those sales paid for the oils and canvas for his portraits. Yes, he was a good painter, but he had very little ambition, and you need that to get your name known. I have some paintings in store, with the rest of his things, but I haven't looked at them since he died.' She turned to her companion. 'Enough about me. Tell me, I'm having a hard time working out whether you're English or French—your accent gives me no clue. I think I'll go for English, because your car has a right-hand drive.'

Francis Morin turned a mock-horrified face her way and tut-tutted reproachfully. 'I'll not answer to being English! I'm half French and half Scottish. My mother is French and lives mostly in Paris since my father died ten years ago.' He slowed the car and swung the wheel over, driving through the open-gated entrance, saying, 'And here we are at the Rousards'.'

How annoying that they had arrived, thought Philippa, wanting to know more. Talking freely about herself had been relaxing. Now there was silence between them again and she was once more conscious of a slight nervousness tinged with excitement rising up in her.

The Spider slid behind two cars already parked. Beyond the courtyard, through a stone arch, was the walled garden where that afternoon Philippa had taken tea with Sylvie. To the right was the house, typically French, with its square blue roofs and rounded turrets.

In the silence after the engine died, Philippa could hear the monotonous chirping of the cicadas and she turned her head and found Francis watching her. He was in no hurry to move and beneath his regard she found her hard-won composure beginning to disintegrate.

'Why were you crying this afternoon, Philippa?'

Whatever she had expected it certainly was not this. She turned and stared out front. 'I wasn't crying.'

'There were tears on your lashes.'

She managed a laugh. 'I was indulging in self-pity. You caught me out.'

'Not something, I'm sure, that you do often.'

'No.' She looked at him then.

'You were annoyed that I caught you at such a vulnerable moment.'

There was a heady fascination being the subject of his concern. Philippa gave a rueful laugh. 'Yes, I was.'

'Do you need help?'

'No, really, it's just a decision I have to make.'

'But perhaps there's a faithful swain back in England who should be asking you that question—ready to share your ups and downs?'

The silence seemed heavy with unspoken words. She lifted her head and looked at him. 'No,' she said simply. And then, 'Does Lisette share yours?'

There was a glimmer of a smile in his eyes. 'You're mixing me up with Jules—it happens all

the time.' He gave a wicked smile and she found
herself smiling back.

When he opened the passenger door for her to
alight a curious feeling swept over her, as if the
step she was about to take was far bigger than
merely lifting her feet from the car to the paving
stones. Giving herself a mental shake, Philippa
accepted his steadying hand, wondering if he was
as sensitive to her touch as she was to his. Long
after contact was broken she could still feel the
imprint and thrust her hand into her skirt pocket
out of harm's way. Walking towards the house
they did not speak.

Fabien came to meet them, a smile of greeting
on his face. A small man with wispy brown hair
and intelligent eyes behind rimless glasses, he had
a quiet gentle manner and a sweet smile. He took
her hands, saying warmly,

'Philippa, my dear, how charming you look.'
His eyes went beyond her. 'Thank you, Francis,
for being a taxi service. There was a crisis at the
hospital which delayed me.'

The drawling voice behind her said, 'It was no
hardship, Fabien,' and Fabien laughed, replying,
'No, I don't suppose it was. No need to put the
jacket on,' he added, as Francis began to do so,
'it's much too warm and we're informal tonight
among our friends.' He waited while his guests
went before him up the steps to the terrace. 'We're
sitting outside as it's such a lovely evening. I have
a new wine I want you to try, Francis, it has an
interesting flavour,' and to Philippa, 'Sylvie will be
down in a moment. She's settling Angélique, who
seems to know that we're having friends in and
wishes to join us.' His voice was lovingly
indulgent.

The terrace was shaded from one end by a bamboo blind, and as the threesome approached, the hum of conversation from the guests already there died down and faces turned their way.

'You all know Francis,' announced Fabien.

'Once seen never forgotten,' quipped a dark-haired man, and everyone laughed.

'So he needs no introduction,' Fabien continued, 'but you don't know Philippa Ingram, an old friend of Sylvie's who is here on holiday from England.' Introductions were set in motion. There were ten guests present, but only two names made any impression on Philippa. The first was Jules Morin, the dark-haired man who had just spoken, and the woman, Lisette, last seen leaving the Orange theatre with Francis Morin.

It was obvious that Lisette recognised Philippa. She gave the English girl a languid greeting in contrast to the sudden narrowing of her dark, thickly lashed eyes. She was dressed in a figure-hugging black dress and close to was even more beautiful than Philippa remembered.

Jules put a drink into Philippa's hand and found her a chair, and even as she responded to the talk around her she was aware that Francis had slowly made his way to the corner of the terrace and was now leaning against the wooden railing. She had to make a conscious effort not to look at him.

Sylvie breezed in, trailing pale green chiffon, her dark curls bouncing as she turned this way and that smiling and greeting her guests. She spied her friend and exclaimed, 'Oh, good, you've arrived, Phippy.' She turned to Francis. 'Thank you, Francis, you were a dear to fetch her for us.'

Francis inclined his head, accepting the thanks, an amused gleam in his eyes. Philippa, attuned to her friend, gave her a closer look. Although in total command of herself, underneath Sylvie was flustered, Philippa could tell. What, she thought, is going on?

Jules appeared at Philippa's side. He was as dark as his cousin was fair and had a much more flamboyant personality. 'May I congratulate you on your command of our language?' He gave her glass a refill.

'Phippy is a language genius,' asserted Sylvie proudly, slipping an arm around her friend's shoulder as she perched on the arm of the chair. 'I could hardly cope with my mother tongue, but Phippy romped away with all the language prizes in the school!'

'Sylvie is exaggerating, as usual,' broke in Philippa. Jules asked, 'Do you use your languages in your job?'

Philippa nodded. She could see the sulky Lisette looking their way.

'She translates books, and goes to conferences and has done *French for Beginners* on television, and made an Italian tape . . .'

Philippa laughingly interrupted her friend. 'Sylvie would make a good agent!'

'How many languages do you have?' asked Jules, and Philippa wondered why he was taking the trouble to get to know her.

'French, Italian and Spanish well enough to use in my job, enough German to get by and a little Dutch.' She smiled, giving a small shrug. 'It's easy if you're that way inclined.'

Fortunately the conversation swun away from her as Lisette called Jules to her side to satisfy some point under discussion from that end of the terrace. Jules excused himself and Philippa sat back, sipping her wine and listening to what was going on around her. Eventually her eyes wandered to the corner.

A shaft of dying sunlight splintered through the blind, catching the pale wheaten hair and turning it to gold. There was unconscious artistic line in the way his body was set against the railing, a wine glass held delicately between long fingers. Robert Ingram had, through his paintings, taught his daughter to appreciate body line, and she wished she had the skill to transpose what she could see on to paper. François ... Francis ... A shiver snaked its way down her spine. It was a long, long time since she had been so attracted to someone with such instant intensity. There—it was voiced! Francis Morin attracted her physically and mentally, and this attraction was not one-sided, she knew that too.

His expression at the moment was a little austere as he gazed down at his wine, and then Fabien approached to refill the glass and stayed to talk, and a smile appeared, softening his features as he listened to his friend.

The time to run—if that's what you want to do—is now, Philippa told herself calmly, before it's too late to turn back. Provide a blinding headache and get Fabien to take you home, if you don't fancy playing with fire.

Sylvie gave a little clap of the hands and called, 'Food is ready, so do, please, go through into the house.'

Her guests obeyed and began to wander inside, still talking to each other, and by dint of manoeuvring tactics Sylvie managed to pull Philippa to one side, whispering urgently,

'He's the wrong one, Phippy!'

Philippa, puzzled, whispered back, 'Who is?'

'Francis! I asked Jules here for you tonight, not Francis!'

'That's very kind of you, Sylvie, but I think Lisette would quarrel with you over that little scheme,' advised Philippa, amused.

'I know that *now*,' responded Sylvie crossly. 'Jules rang Fabien to say that Francis had just arrived from London and could he bring him along, with this Lisette person, and of course Fabien said yes, naturally—we like Francis, he's an asset to any party.'

'Well?' queried Philippa.

'Not well at all,' answered Sylvie, crosser than ever. 'If this Lisette is with Jules then you are automatically partnered with Francis, and he is not husband material, whereas Jules . . .'

'He's married already?' Philippa felt her heart stupidly plummet. Oh God, not another married man on the lookout for a few cheap thrills on the side!

'No, no—but he has a reputation.' Sylvie frowned and bit her lip. 'Damn—if I say that, you'll only be more intrigued. He's wildly attractive, but not what I wish for you, Phippy darling,' and her voice ended on a subdued wail.

'Oh, I don't know,' murmured Philippa mischievously. 'I wouldn't mind him being gift-wrapped and addressed to me.'

'Yes, yes, as an affair of the heart he is well enough, and no stranger to such a thing— naturally, he is a man after all, and discreet.' Sylvie broke off as Fabien turned back to see what was keeping them, his face enquiring. 'Yes, Fabien darling, we are coming,' Sylvie called, and as they began to walk through the house she went on

hurriedly, 'Francis is terribly successful in everything he does and his name has been coupled
many times with various women, but never has
there been someone permanent in his life.' They
were nearly at the dining-room entrance and Sylvie
stopped in her tracks, saying dramatically, 'He
watches you, Phippy, I've noticed—he is attracted
to you, I can tell. He's a terrible heartbreaker,
though I don't think it's his fault, for he never
makes any promises—but I've put him next to you
at table!'

'He's hardly going to break my heart over
dinner, Sylvie love,' soothed Philippa. 'I promise
to be very careful and not to let him seduce me
between courses.'

Sylvie reluctantly laughed and heaved a sigh.
'Very well, I've warned you.'

I need no warning, reflected Philippa as she
followed her friend into the dining-room, where
the glitter of silver, the blood red candles and their
flickering flames and the highly polished table set
the tone for the rest of the evening. It was one that
Philippa was to remember.

Extension leaves had been added to the dining-
table and folding doors opened up so that the
table actually took over two rooms. The women
were already seated and the men were standing,
waiting for their hostess to arrive. Fabien held the
chair at one end of the table for his wife, and
Philippa made for the other vacant place between
the Morin cousins.

Jules pulled back her chair with a flourish and she
shot him a quick smile of thanks. When seated she
took a deep, steadying breath and turned to Francis,
to find amusement gleaming in those shrewd blue
eyes, almost as if he knew of Sylvie's warnings.

Oh dear, oh dear, thought Philippa, her resolve to be cool rapidly disintegrating as he smiled and offered her wine.

The cousins were a formidable duo. By half-way through the evening Philippa's ribs ached with laughing. The one was a perfect foil for the other, and it was as if they had set their stall out to entertain her. Jules was the lighthearted comic, Francis the droll cynic, and they slipped into their double act with the ease of many years' practice.

The general conversation was stimulating and not averse to becoming slightly heated, but only in the way that is possible among close friends. Politics both sides of the Channel were given punishing blows, music was discussed, art and books argued over. Philippa had not enjoyed herself like this in a long time, and the *sotto voce* remarks either side of her at pertinent moments threatened her composure more than once.

Over some delicious local cheeses and while cutting a stem of lush green grapes for Philippa from the fruit platter, Jules asked,

'Do you find you have a dual personality when you come over here? I understand you spent your formative years in France. Do you have difficulty relating to which country you belong?' He dropped the cluster of grapes on to her plate. 'Francis says it is not difficult, that he slips easily into being what is expected of him. In Provence no one thinks of him as being any other than French. How do you find it?'

Philippa thought for a moment. A serious Jules was not to be brushed lightly aside and the question interested her. She said slowly,

'When I first went to England I felt a little strange, but not for long, as I remember. You see,

I spoke without an accent—we always talked together in English, my parents and I, and I have an English name, so people there just accepted me. Oxford is a world of its own anyway. As for France . . .' She frowned. 'I think we were always considered foreigners, looking back, even though we spoke French and lived the life of the locals. There was such a cosmopolitan community around us too. As a child I liked to think myself as being French because I didn't want to be different. As an adult I feel very English with special French roots.'

'I'm glad you like our country.' Jules smiled at her, his dark eyes approving. Philippa wondered what Lisette, on the other side of Francis, was thinking of the seating arrangements.

'I love it,' she answered enthusiastically. 'I'm not here as much as I like to be, that's why I've made a great effort to come this time and stay longer than I usually do.' She held out her glass for a refill and Jules obliged. 'I've brought work with me, so unfortunately it's not all holiday.'

'Francis visits us regularly, but always for brief spells. This time he, too, has a little longer than usual. He's been working too hard and needs to forget his responsibilities. It would be a great kindness if you could look after him during his stay.'

'My dear Jules, I wish you would mind your own business,' came the drawling request from her other side. 'I am quite capable of arranging my own life, thank you,' and Francis turned a bland face to his cousin.

'Indeed he is,' came in Philippa smoothly. 'I think you will find that he is being looked after perfectly adequately. Perhaps you should ask your

cousin how he enjoyed his visit to the Roman
theatre at Orange this afternoon.' She directed this
suggestion to Jules who, with quickening interest,
repeated, 'Roman theatre?' with amused anticipation. Philippa, enjoying herself, turned to
Francis, finding him selecting cheese with due
seriousness.

'Roman theatre?' interrupted Sylvie sharply,
catching the words in a lull and sending a piercing
look across the table. 'At Orange?'

'Why, yes, Sylvie, at Orange,' agreed Francis
calmly.

'*You* were there this afternoon?' demanded
Sylvie, her eyes going quickly to her friend.
Philippa gave a rueful grimace and Sylvie caught
her breath, her mind racing over the conversation
with Philippa that afternoon. Ravishing man—
fair, slim, aristocratic, bright blue eyes! Oh dear,
oh dear! She said, 'I didn't know they allowed
dogs in the theatre.'

'Dogs?' echoed Jules, alive to something going
on and determined to know what it was.

'Yes,' answered Sylvie, with wide-eyed inno-
cence. 'Francis, did you see an Afghan hound there?
On a chain, wasn't he, Phippy? Let me see, how
did you describe him? Aristocratic, sleek and silky,
a bit superior, fair with bright blue eyes, I think
that was it. He sounds very dangerous.'

'Blue eyes? Dogs don't have blue eyes!' This
came from Lisette who had, at first, been talking
to the guest on her other side, but whose ears had
pricked up at the mention of Orange. 'I did not see
any dog there, did you, Francis?' Her manner was
slightly scornful and she shot Philippa an irritable
look.

Philippa, a pang of dismay shooting through

her, suddenly remembered that Lisette was Jules'
girl-friend and she swung her head round
anxiously to see his reaction. Her worries
disappeared as she met the laughter dancing in his
eyes.

'You took *Lisette* to the Roman theatre at
Orange, Francis?' Jules asked, allowing just the
hint of surprise to touch his voice. 'I'm sure she
was fascinated by it.'

'It was very interesting,' muttered Lisette, and
tossed her dark curls and studiously turned her
back on him.

'Lisette wished to drive the Spider and offered
to accompany me,' put in Francis mildly,
dropping his voice for his cousin alone, although
with Philippa sitting between them she was
bound to hear, 'and she wanted a shoulder to
cry on.' He lifted a brow. 'I do wish your
love-life was not so volcanic, Jules, it makes
things complicated.'

Jules grinned unrepentantly and conversation
resumed round the table, and after a suitable
interval an amused voice on Philippa's right said,

'So you liken me to an Afghan hound, do you?'

Philippa turned her head and met his gaze. 'You
should be flattered.'

A laugh trembled on his voice. 'Oh, my dear, I
am. I've been called many things in my time. Such
a beautiful animal, with a prestigious pedigree,
makes a change. I admit to being a little concerned
about the superior bit, but really . . .! On a chain?'
and he regarded her reproachfully.

'I see now I was mistaken,' Philippa replied
kindly, 'although the role of Dutch uncle is not
one I can easily see you in.'

'And what role do you see me in?' The question

was lazily put, but the blue eyes narrowed thoughtfully.

Philippa gave a small laugh and shook her head. 'Oh, no! I won't commit myself on such a short acquaintance.' Her eyes slid past him and rested momentarily upon Lisette. 'She is very attractive.'

'Yes, she is, isn't she?' agreed Francis, 'but not really interested in Roman remains—or Shakespeare.' His mouth curved and try as she might Philippa could not stop her own from trembling in answer. She caught her bottom lip between her teeth, fought a losing battle, and asked resignedly,

'What has Shakespeare got to do with it?'

'They are performing *A Midsummer Night's Dream* there next week. I went to buy two tickets. It's rather a good setting for fairies and magic, enchantment and romance, don't you think?' He speared some cheese with his knife and then turned his eyes her way. 'Will you come with me?'

A nerve fluttered in her throat and Philippa looked away, almost immediately returning to find his regard still upon her.

'Yes, please,' she said, burning her boats. His response was a quick smile and a quiet, 'Good,' and then they were drawn into other talk.

It was arranged that Fabien would take her home. No doubt Sylvie's doing—she had been eyeing them all evening, and if Sylvie was surprised that Francis made no move to offer himself in Fabien's place she did not show it.

Philippa was content. She needed to catch her breath. Was it only that afternoon that she had confessed to never having fallen so much in love that she lost all sense? Fate must have laughed out loud! Not that she had fallen in love—good heavens, that was much too over-dramatic, but she had a strong presentiment that she was heading into some emotional involvement. There was something about this slim, fair man that pulled at her senses, and the suddenness was alarming. It seemed to her that everyone in the room had become more animated, more interesting and attractive because of his presence. That was what was so panicky. That she could think such romantic twaddle—she who was usually so pragmatic. After all, she was not a silly young thing to be swept off her feet by a pair of smiling blue eyes and a drawling voice. She was a sensible woman of twenty-seven who was independent and answerable to no one. So it was unnerving, to say the least, to find herself flapping around exactly like a silly young thing.

Before leaving, she looked in on Angélique. The light from the landing shone faintly across the curve of a glowing cheek, eyelashes that trembled slightly and sweetly shaped, out-thrust bottom lip. As Philippa stood gazing down on to the sleeping child a shadow joined her, causing her to put a finger to her lips, and for a moment they stood together, sharing the intimate occasion, then they made their way quietly from the room.

'Your shawl was downstairs. It had dropped to the floor.' Francis held up the lost shawl as evidence and inclined his head towards the nursery. 'She's aptly named at the moment.'

Philippa chuckled and they began to descend the stairs. 'Angélique? Yes, she is, isn't she? My knowledge of small babies is very nearly nil— Angel is the only one I come into real contact with, and she's my goddaughter. And you?'

'The Morin family is large,' he admitted,

smiling. He dropped the shawl round her shoulders, taking care not to touch her. 'Have you anything planned for tomorrow?'

Philippa shook her head. Do not, she told herself sternly, look too pleased.

'Have you done any canoeing?'

She found herself smiling. Canoeing was hardly soft lights and sweet music and seduction! 'In my childhood,' she admitted. 'Why do you ask?'

'We'll canoe down the Ardèche. It's quite impressive. I'll call for you at nine-thirty.'

Two arms encircled her from behind and a growly voice asked, 'Would you like a chaperone, Philippa? I could always take the day off.'

'You can paddle your own canoe, cousin,' said Francis, and Jules grinned and kissed her on both cheeks as he said good night.

Francis neither kissed her, nor took her hand.

CHAPTER THREE

THE drive back to Villeneuve-lès-Avignon seemed a perfect opportunity to pump Fabien for some information.

Fabien was innocently forthcoming. 'Francis? I've known him ever since I can remember—he's part of my boyhood, along with Jules and a handful of others. The Morins are an extraordinary family and Francis is no exception ... nothing seems to daunt him, he'll try his hand at anything in his quiet way, and usually succeeds. He keeps success and failure close to his chest and he's a good man to have around. He's one of the few people I could go to if I were ever in real trouble—he'd help and ask no questions.'

'What does he do?' asked Philippa curiously, and Fabien laughed a little.

'Difficult question. He read science at university which led him into electronics. You should get him to tell you how today's high technology will transform our lives—amazing stuff! Do you realise that by the turn of the century, lasers could replace the silicone chip altogether? That's because light travels much faster than electrons.' He laughed, adding, 'Or so Francis was telling me tonight.'

'But he's involved in more than that?' prompted Philippa, her interest and respect growing.

Fabien gave a little nod of the head. 'I believe he inherited shares from his father, something to do with the wool industry, and, of course, the family firm which makes glass, and he's on the board of directors of a couple of firms here in Provence to my knowledge, and probably in England too. He's always dashing off to some place or another, but he doesn't talk about himself much. Jules reckons the secret of his success is that he has the right amount of nerve to take a gamble when it's necessary. In a funny sort of way, his father made Francis what he is today.'

'How do you mean?'

'From what I can gather, he and his father were different as chalk and cheese. Francis has a keen brain and likes to use it. His father sat back and expected the family business to take care of itself, speculating badly on the Stock Exchange, and his marriage wasn't working. Hélène Morin didn't transplant easily to your northern shores—Jules says family opinion was that they should never have married—but Hélène isn't the kind of woman to give in without trying. After her husband's death . . .'

'How was that?'

'Broke his neck on the hunting field, if I remember right, and afterwards Hélène made Paris her permanent home. She rarely goes to England now and runs a very successful antique business. Luckily Francis inherited her energy and intelligence and has brought the family business into prominence again.'

'I wonder why he isn't married?' Philippa murmured.

'I asked him that myself recently and he said he hadn't time! That's nonsense, of course, and he didn't expect to be taken seriously. I don't suppose his parents' unhappiness has helped, one's not so quick to tie oneself down with such a background, and his work has something to do with it too, he's a busy man.' He laughed. 'His lady friends are slotted into his life to suit Francis.'

'And there's no shortage,' broke in Philippa drily, and Fabien shrugged eloquently.

Philippa wondered if she was prepared to be slotted into Francis Morin's life. Fabien was silent as they re-crossed the Daladier Bridge, the lights of Villeneuve twinkling ahead of them.

'It has just occurred to me,' he announced suddenly, sounding pleased with himself, 'you should get Francis to take you around, Philippa, show you the sights. You've never stayed long enough to explore much, have you, and Francis is on holiday and knows Provence well.'

Philippa hid a smile. 'That's quite an idea, Fabien.' Ye gods! she thought, how Sylvie would scream if she could hear her husband at this minute! Dear, sweet Fabien . . .

Francis Morin arrived on the dot of nine-thirty, as Philippa suspected he would, and had given her cotton top and matching shorts with their cover-up skirt an approving glance. He was not to know that it was the third set of clothing she had put on since getting up. He looked even more approving when she told him she was wearing a swim-suit underneath, adding, 'Just in case I take a ducking.'

'Oh, I shall take better care of you than that, I hope,' he replied, smiling lazily. 'And a woman who can be ready on time! How promising!' They stood for a moment, eyeing each other over the Spider's roof, and the same challenging sparks began to flow between them.

'That's a typical male observation,' said Philippa, and the smile broadened.

'Yes, isn't it? Shall we go?'

The Ardèche Gorge was impressive. To get to
the starting point for their journey down river it
was necessary to drive through the mountain
pass, with the occasional glimpses of the river
twisting its way far below. Every now and then,
Francis would stop the car at a vantage point
and he and Philippa would get out and walk to
the edge. The views were breathtaking and a
little frightening.

At the Pont d'Arc, a massive natural archway
hewn out of rock by the force of the river and
elements, Francis arranged for the Spider to be
driven back to await them at the end of their
journey down river. Money changed hands and
they climbed down the steep path to the river's
edge. There was a small launching beach and soon
they were afloat.

'We needn't be energetic,' Francis told her,
paddle laid across the bows as he turned to
speak to her. 'The river is going the same way as
we are.' He gave a lopsided grin. 'If we capsize,
first rescue priority is lunch,' and he indicated a
canvas grip he had placed neatly in the centre of
the canoe.

The Ardèche wound its way between the giant
towering cliffs, sometimes in sunshine, sometimes
in shade. After an hour's paddling, Francis
pointed to an inlet similar to one of the many
they had already passed and they steered their
way towards it. Having stripped off his slacks at
the start, revealing dark navy swim trunks, and
with canvas shoes on his feet, Francis now
jumped into the shallow water and angled the
canoe between the jagged rocks until Philippa
could gain the beach without a wetting. They
pulled the canoe out of the water and stood,

breathing a little heavily, and exchanged smiles of satisfaction.

'Well done, First Officer. Shall we swim before lunch?'

'Aye, aye, Skipper.'

All very juvenile, but fun. Francis did not look at all juvenile, however, when he stripped off his sports shirt and stood waiting for Philippa to rid herself of her own clothes. As she did so she was very much aware of the slim, compact frame and lots of bare, tanned flesh only a few feet away. Now down to her coral bathing suit, a one-piece, beautifully cut and boasting a horrendous price tag, she was determined not to feel self-conscious. Tossing away the shorts, aiming them to drop neatly on to the already discarded skirt and top, she straightened and met his eyes, her expression slightly on the defensive.

Francis said easily, 'Beware hidden rocks,' and strolled down to the river's edge. Relieved, she followed and waded in, stepping carefully. The water was cold. Philippa's breath left her on first contact, but she had always accepted any reasonable challenge and set out with a clean stroke, making for the other side of the river. Francis kept up with her, stroke for stroke, although she guessed he could have overtaken her. As the water became more shallow they made for a rock and hauled themselves on to it to take a breather. When Philippa began to shiver, Francis said, 'Time to go back. Make for that rock a little higher up from our beach—see it? The current might take you further down if you're not aware of what's happening. I'll keep down river of you. Ready?'

Philippa nodded, took a breath and slid in. She

could see what he meant. The pull was quite strong now that they were going slightly against the flow. She was not sorry when she found she could put her feet to the bottom.

Taking her hand and pulling her up the sand, Francis smiled and said, 'Good girl!' and she felt a ridiculous pleasure sweep over her.

'What would you have done if I couldn't have made it?' she asked curiously.

He threw her a towel and took another from the grip and began to briskly dry himself. 'We would have drifted with the river and landed further down, then climbed back over the rocks.' He straightened and gave his hair a quick rub, then added, 'I always try to be one step ahead,' and regarded her thoughtfully for a second before smiling.

Philippa caught her breath. That smile just wasn't fair! 'Is that a threat or a promise?' she asked, and found herself returning the smile.

'I hope,' said Francis, stepping forward and dabbing the towel across her shoulders, where she had missed drying herself, 'that it's a promise. Let's eat.'

The grip produced a baguette, pâté, goat's cheese, large juicy tomatoes and wine in a flask to keep cool.

'How marvellously domesticated you are!' exclaimed Philippa with teasing admiration. It was a useful protection against the expanse of freckled chest and even browner length of arms and legs only a touch away. His hair had a tendency to wave when wet.

'I like the simple things in life,' he admitted with the drawl she was coming to expect. As he poured the wine into one of the flask's tops, he added casually, 'Do you suppose Sylvie is up above, eyeing us through binoculars?' His brows rose exaggeratedly and Philippa burst out laughing.

'No, no, Sylvie can't stand heights,' she assured him soothingly, her eyes brimming with amusement.

'And I thought Sylvie was my friend,' he complained, full of hurt.

'You have a reputation.' Philippa bit into the crusty bread, waiting for his reply, enjoying herself.

'Really? She thinks you need to be protected from me?' The idea obviously pleased him.

Pausing before taking a drink, Philippa asked, 'Isn't she right?' then allowed the cool, sparkling liquid to trickle down her throat. It was a provocative pose, but one she could not help. Everything she did seemed to be provocative, so aware was she of her body when she was in his company. Eyes closed, the sun beating on to her bare flesh, she could see in her mind's eye the mass of damp, springing waves of her hair, red-gold where the sun had kissed it, spilling down her back. Could see the tilted profile—the curve of throat, the drying swim-suit with grains of sand clinging to the shiny material, the swell of her breasts, the curve of her hips, her legs, one outstretched, the other arched at the knee.

And if she were completely truthful, deep down in her heart of hearts, she wanted Francis to like what he could see.

She heard him say calmly, 'Of course Sylvie's right. The point is, do you want to be protected?'

She opened her eyes and put down the drink. Francis was sitting with his arms round updrawn knees, hands loosely clasped, eyes resting pensively upon her. He seemed to be very relaxed. Philippa envied him his self-control.

With the pulse throbbing in her neck and warmth rising to her face, she said, 'No, I don't,' and after a moment, heightened by a frisson of expectancy charging the air between them, Francis said softly, 'Good,' and leaned forward and touched his lips to hers, very, very gently.

As he drew back he murmured, 'You taste of wine—delicious! Can I tempt you with an orange? I'll peel it for you,' and the moment, brief and exquisite, was put aside.

'Tell me about your family,' demanded Francis lightly, stretching out on his back, hands behind his head.

'Not much to tell,' replied Philippa, offering an orange segment. 'I don't know the Ingrams, and the only Stanhope I have anything to do with is my mother's sister, Grace. She has a house in Wimbledon which is divided into two flats and I live in the upstairs one.'

'What do you mean, you don't know the Ingrams?'

'Just that. I've never met them. They live in Cumbria.' She shrugged. 'I've not missed them. My father left home and never returned after a row with his father.'

'Aren't you curious about them?' asked Francis.

Philippa reached for the towel and wiped her hands free of orange juice. 'To my surprise I find I am.'

'Why surprise?'

'Well, you see ...' She stopped and pulled a face. 'I don't want to bore you with my family history ...'

'I'm quite capable of changing the subject,'

drawled Francis, and Philippa considered this statement and said cheerfully,

'You've been warned.' She hugged her knees and gazed thoughtfully across the river. 'It's the old, old story of a father trying to impose his will on to his son—my grandfather wanted my father to go into the family business. The Ingrams founded Copperthwaite Mills years ago and make cloth, rather good stuff actually. The idea of Robert in a factory situation is mind-boggling, but he left school and dutifully went to the Mills to learn the trade from the bottom up and hated it, because all he wanted to do was paint. My grandfather was an obstinate man, from all accounts. He had already lost one son, Father's elder brother, in a drowning accident, and all his hopes were on Father. I can understand that, but you can't live your children's lives for them, can you?'

Francis said, 'No, of course you can't.'

'And then, to complicate things further, Father met Mother. She was, according to my aunt, beautiful. I can only remember her when she was ill, but at nineteen, when Father met her, she was lovely. To a painter, and one whose interest was in portraiture, she was perfection—lovely bones, transparent skin, pale green eyes and dark brown hair the colour of a matured conker. How could Father resist her?'

'I gather he didn't.' Francis eyed her. 'Are you like your mother?'

Philippa laughed. 'Unfortunately no. I have her bone structure, but not her constitution, for which I'm grateful, and her mop of hair, but not the colour, which is infuriating. The rest is pure Ingram, including, according to Grace, the Ingram stubbornness.' She wrinkled her nose speculatively. 'Dad told my grandfather that he wasn't interested in wool, that he was going to paint, and that he was going to marry Rose—my mother. There was an almighty row and that was that.' She allowed sand to trickle through her fingers and went on slowly, 'My grandfather was a fool. He should have realised that, for all his easy ways, Dad was as stubborn as himself, but he didn't, and it's stupid to issue ultimatums. They always backfire.'

Francis leaned up on one elbow, saying, 'He probably would agree with you.'

'I think Mother could have put things right eventually, given the chance. She was so sweet-natured and kind, but they moved to France for her health just after I was born and never returned to England.'

Francis sat up and began to brush the sand from his back. 'Shall you eventually satisfy your curiosity about the Ingrams, do you think?'

'The opportunity does seem to have offered itself,' Philippa admitted, and told him about the birthday invitation. 'The need to know one's roots seems to grow as the years pass.'

'So you'll go.'

She looked at him and gave a little laugh. 'Yes, I'll go.' She tilted her head. 'You sure have a knack of making me talk! What about your family?'

'Very thin over in England, extremely prolific over here.' He grinned. 'What I lack in siblings I gain in cousins, although Jules is more like a brother.' He twisted round and peered upwards, assessing the position of the sun. 'We're going to be blocked out in a minute and the time's getting on anyway, so my family will have to wait.'

They packed up the picnic things and pulled clothing over their by now dry swimsuits. It was incredible, thought Philippa, how the time had flown, and even more so how happy she was. So far there had been no discordant note in their relationship, no rushing of fences, and she liked that. And they had talked, arguing amicably over some things, during the car journey. It was a relief to find a man who did not want to dominate her with his opinions. It was a delightful experience knowing she was being drawn more and more under his spell and not resisting.

As they set off down river she feasted her eyes on him with no fear of discovery. The cotton shirt straining at the seams as he drove the paddle deep into the water showed the strength across his shoulders. There were droplets of water clinging to his arms and the ruffled buttermilk hair drew colour from the sun.

How amazing when I'm not usually attracted to fair men, she thought, smiling to herself.

When Francis threw back the occasional glance or remark, she allowed her happiness to show on her face and didn't give a damn. The small, sly voice inside her head that still insisted she was playing with dynamite, she drowned in the waters of the Ardèche without scruple.

At St Martin the gorge widened, and it was here that they handed in the canoe and collected the Spider.

'Tired?' asked Francis, turning to her as they drove off, and she answered, 'Mmm . . . pleasantly so.'

'What would you like to do now?' Francis looked at the dash clock and went on, 'I know an inn, off the main road south of Bagnols, which has a good chef and a pianist who sings the best jazz and blues in the district.'

'Sounds just right—so long as there's the means to wash and brush up. I hope it's not too grand? I feel a mess.'

'It's a very casual place, but you need have no fears, you look——' he gave her a brief glance, paused slightly, and went on,'——delightful.'

'That wasn't the word you were going to use,' accused Philippa, laughing, lifting up a strand of hair. 'Could it have been windswept that first came to mind?'

'I was going to say adorable,' Francis replied tranquilly.

Philippa shot him a swift look, faint pink colouring her cheeks. She let out a feeble 'Oh.'

'*I* am quite happy with adorable, but it may be too soon for you. I have to keep reminding myself that we only met yesterday ... so I'll settle for delightful.'

There seemed to be no answer to that, and Philippa hugged adorable to herself in secret.

As it was fairly early the inn was only sparsely scattered with diners. Francis was greeted with enthusiasm by the *patron* and they were shown to a table by the window which overlooked a pretty courtyard.

'Speciality of the house today is rabbit—*Sauté de Lapin aux Pruneaux*—have you a liking for rabbit with prunes?' Francis asked, lifting his eyes from the menu, eyes teasing.

'I'll let you know,' promised Philippa loftily, and he raised his brows and drawled,

'She's on time, she's delightfully adorable and ready to try *lapin aux pruneaux*! The gods are laughing! Or you could have fish, duck or ...'

'Rabbit,' broke in Philippa firmly. 'Never let it be said I was a quitter!'

The dish was delicious. The chef came to speak with them and informed Philippa that it was a country dish from Picardy, where he himself had been born. He begged to be allowed to bring Mademoiselle a crêpe which he would create in her honour. He beamed a smile when she accepted his offer and a few moments later the chafing dish and table burner were brought forward and with considerable interest from the rest of the diners Crêpe Philippa was created. Invited to take a taste, Philippa gave her wholehearted approval and the chef, satisfied, bustled back to his kitchen.

Francis, who had refused dessert, sat back in his chair watching her, occasionally sipping his claret.

'A healthy appetite too,' he murmured, adding to his list, and Philippa, spoon poised, said indignantly,

'So I should think! Canoeing is strenuous work, you know!' She finished the last mouthful and groaned, 'Absolutely gorgeous . . . I couldn't eat another thing. How grand to have a pudding named after oneself!'

'Crêpe Suzette was inspired by a *petite amie* of Edward VII when he was Prince of Wales,' offered Francis, eyes gleaming.

Philippa widened her own. 'Really? What snippets of information you do have!' She dropped the bantering and said quietly, 'Thank you, Francis, for today . . . it has been lovely.'

'I'm glad. Perhaps you'll allow me to be your guide tomorrow?' He saw hesitation cross her face and said quickly, 'But you have something else planned. Never mind, another day . . .?'

'No, I have nothing planned,' she said, and

raised her eyes to his, and they contemplated each
other for a second or two that had no hurry and
she said simply, 'Where shall we go?'

When the following day's itinerary had been
discussed Francis said casually, 'I have to fly to
Bonn on Friday on business.'

'I thought Jules said you were on holiday?'
Damn! Had she shown too much disappointment?

'I am, but Bonn is something I can't put off. I'll
be there four days, but I'll be back in time to take
you to see the play,' promised Francis, very
content to hear the disappointment.

Provence, in the days that followed, became
touched with magic. They explored its treasures,
driving the Spider up into the hills to seek out tiny
villages perched upon craggy cliffs. They dis-
covered gaily coloured harbours full of fishing
boats, wide graceful avenues, churches and village
squares. They watched *pétanque*, the game of
bowls played with deadly seriousness by men
young and old, gave their considered opinion on
several wines and when Francis had to leave for
Bonn, Philippa resigned herself to the work she
should have been doing anyway. She found it
difficult to concentrate and more often than not
ended up calling on Sylvie.

On the fourth day of his absence Sylvie
remarked drily, 'It seems that the ton of bricks has
fallen.'

Philippa, who was gazing absently out of the
window, gave a short laugh. 'It has.'

'I hope you know what you're doing, Phippy,'
Sylvie said with some anxiety, and Philippa
returned ruefully,

'I'm not doing anything, as yet.'

'Which proves he has patience,' declared Sylvie,

adding quickly, 'Sorry, sorry—I hereby resign from being mother hen!'

Philippa flapped a forgiving hand. 'You don't say anything I haven't said to myself, Sylvie. I've held back, really I have, but it's no good. These four days have seemed like four months. I can't believe it's happening to me! I can't describe what it's like being with him and I feel only half alive when he's away.' Philippa gave a groaning laugh. 'Hell, how banal I sound! He's a rag-bag of information, he makes me laugh, he knows when to talk and when to listen—I've talked more about myself to him than to any other living soul apart from you—his intellect appeals to me and . . .' She stopped short.

'He's physically attractive to you,' finished Sylvie. 'You could be in love.'

'You do like him, don't you, Sylvie?' asked Philippa a little urgently, unable to look at her friend as she asked.

'I've always liked him, Phippy, he's an old friend of Fabien's. I just don't want you to be hurt, that's all.'

'Why should I be?' demanded Philippa, and frowned. 'I might be,' she conceded, 'who can tell? Anyway, I don't care.'

Sylvie sighed. 'Yes, you're in love.'

Francis returned. There was no ignoring the implosion of pleasure she felt when she opened the door to him. She was careful not to show how much she had missed him but, if anything, the four days' absence seemed to strengthen their rapport. They went to Orange and watched Shakespeare's lighthearted play about fairies and crossed lovers, and to Philippa, she and Francis seemed to be living in a similar enchantment. She knew there was no turning back, and that he held her happiness in his hands.

The next morning found them speeding south towards the Camargue, the district where the River Rhône empties out into the sea. There was a festival held every year at a town on the coast called Les Saintes Maries de la Mer, which Francis thought Philippa would enjoy.

'The place is named after the three Marys from the gospel,' he told her as he drove. 'Marie Jacobé—she was the sister of the Virgin Mary; Marie Salomé—the mother of James and John; and Mary Magdalene. There's a story attached to them,' he added, and glanced her way.

'Tell me,' urged Philippa lightly. They had greeted each other that morning with the slight wariness of people about to set off on an escapade the outcome of which could turn out to be a mite dangerous. A story could ease things.

'Well,' said Francis, 'all three were at the Crucifixion and according to legend they left Palestine, with Lazarus and Martha and some others, together with a black servant called Sara, in a boat without oars or sails.'

'Without . . .?' You mean they just drifted with the tides and winds right across the Mediterranean?' exclaimed Philippa.

'That's what is said. They landed safely on the coast—miraculously, I suppose, would be the right word, and Marie Jacobé and Marie Salomé stayed, with Sara, and built a small chapel on the site of pagan temple. Later, a church was built on the same spot and later still, when the gipsies began to arrive in Provence in the fifteenth century, they adopted Sara as their patron saint.'

'Do you think it's true?'

'The whole of Provence is a pot-pourri of myth and history, and steeped in so many different religions and races how can legend and history be disentangled?' Francis drew her attention outside. 'See how flat the land is becoming? We're into the delta of the Rhône now.'

Philippa looked out of the window. Miles and miles of marshland spread before her as far as the horizon, the flatness broken only by the occasional clump of trees or church spire. A flock of birds emerged from the long grass and flew low across the marsh, settling into obscurity further away. Glimpses of water could be seen, reflecting the sun, and Francis, following the flight of birds with a quick glance, remarked,

'The authorities have made the marsh into a zoological and botanical nature reserve with stringent rules for protection of the wild life here. The best way to see the Camargue is on horseback. We're staying with my cousin and her husband, who own one of the many ranches dotted around the area.'

Philippa said teasingly, 'Wherever we go there seems to be a Morin cousin!'

Jean and Colette made them welcome, greeting Francis enthusiastically and Philippa with smiling friendliness and an underlying interest, confirmed by Colette's words as she showed Philippa to her bedroom.

'We were delighted to learn that Francis was bringing someone with him.' She walked round the bedroom, on the lookout for anything not quite right. Satisfied, she turned to Philippa, adding, 'He usually comes alone,' and on that piece of information, she left.

Thoughtfully, Philippa unpacked the small case she had brought and changed into a pair of jodhpurs and boots she had borrowed, then wandered over to the window, tucking in her blouse at the waist as she looked out on to the stable yard below. A string of Camargue horses—white to the uninitiated, grey to equestrians—were returning from taking their riders out on an exploration trail of the marshes. Their voices floated upwards, cheerful, with the odd laugh, as they entered the ranch house for refreshment.

A knock on the door and Francis calling her name caused Philippa to hurry. Joining him, she found he was holding two riding hats.

'I want you to put this on,' he said. 'I make it a rule never to ride without one, in case of accidents. It's a bind, especially when it's hot, but I've known too many people either killed or injured for life to ignore the dangers.' He watched critically as Philippa adjusted the chin-strap and then put on his own as he led the way to the stables. The horses were waiting for them, already saddled, and again Francis took time to check the girths and made sure he was completely satisfied before they set off.

He rode behind for a while, obviously assessing Philippa's capability, and then moved up to join her. She looked at him and smiled, saying,

'It's like riding a bike, you never forget, but I reckon I'm going to pay for it tomorrow!'

'There's always payment for everything in some form or another,' Francis responded, throwing her a slightly sardonic smile.

They followed the track for a little under two miles, Francis naming the birds they flushed and reining in his mount brought their leisurely ride to a halt, staring out across the marsh.

'I was here two years ago when the pink flamingoes came through on their way from North America. Ten thousand of them—it was an incredible sight, one I'll never forget. I can't provide flamingoes at the moment, but ...' He stood in the stirrups and put up binoculars. After a moment he handed them over, '... to the right and beyond that clump of bushes. They blend into the landscape, but you can just make them out. A herd of bulls, and a little further on, about thirty wild horses.' He waited while Philippa got them into focus and added, 'There's a *corride* tonight. Shall we go?'

'A bullfight?' Philippa lowered the glasses and turned to him consideringly. 'They don't kill the bull here, do they, so I'll say yes.' She handed back the binoculars and as his hand closed over hers he said teasingly,

'Softhearted Pippa!'

He so rarely touched her that when there was contact it was like an electric shock. Her eyes flew up to his and heat flooded her face.

'You called me Pippa.' She said the first thing that came into her head.

The horses moved impatiently, jostling closer.

'I'm sorry.' Francis frowned and looked down at her hand, still retained in his. 'Would you rather I didn't?'

'No ... my father was ... he called me Pippa,' she offered lamely, and then, 'You may—if you wish.'

He smiled and as the animals moved abruptly the smile took a comical downward turn at the corners and he was forced to let go her hand as his horse side-stepped away. Checking it, he said ruefully, 'This isn't the most practical of places to whisper sweet nothings, is it?'

Philippa burst out laughing and raised her brows, asking lightly, 'Francis Morin, are you making love to me?'

Francis said slowly, 'Balfour, not Morin.' His eyes searched her face as they began to move forward again, seeing the puzzlement she was feeling.

'What do you mean?' she asked.

'You forget that my mother is the Morin. My father was Duncan Balfour, a Scot. My name is Francis Morin Balfour.' He paused. 'I did tell you, I think, that I was half Scot, half French.'

Feeling oddly disconcerted, Philippa replied, 'Yes, I remember you did, but . . .'

'Nothing's changed. I'm still the same person.'

'But I've always thought of you as Francis Morin,' she protested, 'and now I'm going to have to get used to you as Francis Balfour!'

'I don't care how you think of me, so long as you do.' He gave her an amused side-glance. 'If it's any consolation I doubt whether anyone ever thinks of me as Balfour in France. I spent so much time with my cousins that I'm considered to be a Morin.' He checked his watch. 'We've been out long enough, I think. If we take this track we can go back by another route.'

They trotted into the yard some time later and Philippa groaned as Francis walked over to help her dismount.

'I don't think I can get off! Canoeing, swimming and now this. I suspect you're putting me through some sort of secret endurance test!'

Francis threw back his head and roared with

laughter. 'Poor girl, is that what it feels like?' He
held up his hands and clasped her waist and she
slipped off the saddle. As her feet touched the
ground he remained holding her and with a
quizzical look on his face he said, 'The answer to
your question is yes.'

Trying to remember their earlier conversation,
Philippa asked, puzzled, 'What question?'

'Yes, I am making love to you.'

Philippa's mount moved abruptly and bumped
her sharply against his chest and his arms went
round her. With a gasp of surprise she asked, 'Did
you train him to do that?' laughing a little, her
senses quickening.

'To get what I want, nothing is beyond me,'
drawled Francis smugly, then his face changed and
his mouth came down on hers.

The blood pounded in Philippa's ears and every
nerve ending burst into a whoosh of happiness.
She could feel his heart beating as fast and as hard
as her own and her body moulded to his with
incredible perfection.

'Adorable beautiful Pippa!' His voice was
quietly exultant, his breath warm against her face.
'I knew this could happen the moment I set eyes
on you.'

They walked to the house, arms around each
other, and brought in with them an aura of
romance, endorsing Colette's hopes as she watched
them.

That evening they drove into Les Saintes Maries
and wandered through the town, mingling with the
festive crowd. Gipsies, Camargue cowboys, the
fifes and tambours of the musicians, all added to
the noise and gaiety of the dancing and sideshows.

'The gipsies come from all over,' explained

Francis, holding her close so that they could not become separated in the crowd. 'Tonight they'll keep a vigil in the crypt of the church, tomorrow there's a special service in the Saints' honour and a procession carries the statues of the Saints in a model boat down to the shore. The boat will be carried into the waves and the Bishop will bless the sea. The real festivities begin then—Provençal dances, feats of horsemanship, wrestling with the bulls, sideshows—in fact, all the fun of the fair.' He stopped. 'I don't believe you've heard a word I've been saying!'

'Yes, I have,' Philippa protested truthfully, but she had been watching him, as well as listening. The crisp blue shirt accentuated the blue of his eyes. His fair head always drew attention wherever they went, especially female, and tonight was no exception. Philippa was merely enjoying the fact that it was she who was walking in the shelter of his arm and not someone else.

At the *corride* they cheered with the rest of the spectators as competitors tried to secure the red cockade hanging between the horns of the bull with the multi-pronged hook used especially for the purpose. Quite late, they returned to the ranch, and Francis kissed her outside her bedroom door and pushed her gently through. She had known instinctively that he would not come to her while they stayed there.

Colette's approval blossomed and she was very happy to talk about Francis to Philippa in the odd moments they were alone together. Philippa learned that it was Francis who had loaned his cousin the initial down-payment on the ranch and was in no hurry for it to be repaid, preferring to be a partner in the venture.

'So you see, I am prejudiced about him,' admitted Colette, smiling, 'but you know his worth. Francis is loyal to his family and friends. I am so glad he has at last found someone to make him happy. Ah, you blush, but he has never brought anyone with him before,' she said firmly, 'and he is happy. I can tell.'

In the face of such certainty Philippa did not argue and went away to build a few dreams.

The festival over, they left the ranch with the afternoon nearly gone. For some miles there was silence between them and then Francis asked, a trifle abruptly, 'Do you have to return to Villeneuve today?' He glanced briefly her way and when Philippa murmured, 'No,' he turned at the next fork in the road, saying, 'Then I shall take you to Les Baux.'

The terrain was changing. The flat delta was left behind and they began to climb. The road wound its way upwards through a range of arid, craggy hills. On the lower slopes were olive and almond trees, higher up the trees gave way to scrub and coarse grass. The summits of the hills were bare rock.

Les Alpilles. This mountain range had a wild, peculiar haunting quality which appealed to Philippa, and the village of Les Baux remained invisible almost to the last turn of the road. As Francis swung the Spider to a halt she thought the place looked as though it was hewn out of the rock it stood upon.

'You'll understand why we have to leave the car here when you see how narrow the streets are— some of them are even stepped.' He tucked her arm through his as they entered the village through an archway and Philippa looked round her with quickening curiosity. The street they were slowly climbing was extremely narrow and on either side the buildings clung to each other, all built of the same rough grey stone. Tiny windows showed their wares—craft-work, pottery and paintings.

'How old is it?' asked Philippa.

Francies replied, 'Oh, Les Baux goes back to the Iron Age, but it was in the Middle Ages that it came into its own. Stuck up on this peak it's a natural fortress and was owned by one of the most powerful families in southern France—the *seigneurs* of Baux. It was once a notorious bandits' nest.'

'You know such picturesque bits of history,' praised Philippa.

'That's not the reason I've brought you here.'

'No? You have another quaint story for me?'

'If you think troubadours quaint, then yes. It was here that they found their inspiration in what was called the Courts of Love.' Francis was smiling, but she sensed a purpose behind the banter.

'Ah!' she breathed, playing the game. 'The poets with their lutes and lyres, singing songs of gallantry, courtship and chivalry!'

'With the winner receiving a crown of peacocks' feathers and a kiss from the most beautiful lady present.'

They were now standing outside an open doorway, the entrance dropping downwards to accommodate the slope of the mountain.

Philippa's eyes sparkled. 'Why, Francis! Do you feel in good voice? I'm not too sure of the peacocks' feathers, but I've seen a couple of pigeons!' She peered into the dark interior and could just make out a reception desk. 'I wonder if they could provide the lute?' She straightened and turned to face him, and her heart began to beat faster at the look on his face.

Francis said, 'Shall we go in and find out?' and Philippa replied gravely, 'I thought you'd never ask.'

The room was delightful—the furniture old and the double bed canopied. The view from the window scanned the steep slope of the mountain and Francis, withdrawing his head, announced, 'I'm glad I don't have to climb up that to sing you a love song.'

'I'll let down my hair,' promised Philippa.

They went for a walk after their evening meal, finally ending up on the edge of a wide, rock-strewn promontory.

'To watch the sun rise over the southern plain from here is said to be one of the wonders of the world.' Francis narrowed his eyes, peering into the distance. 'On a clear day you can see as far as the coast.' He glanced down at her, his arm tightening, drawing her closer. 'Not cold, are you?'

Philippa shook her head and dug her hands deeper into her jacket pockets. 'No, not really. We're awfully high up here, aren't we? I think it must be the ghosts that are prowling. It's a bit desolate, isn't it?' She looked back over her shoulder to the ruined fortifications, dark grey and sombre in the fading light. 'The whole village is so full of history it positively bristles with ghosts.' She laughed ruefully. 'It probably looks better in sunshine. I'm not usually so sensitive to atmosphere.'

'You have every right to be sensitive just here. It's said,' Francis informed her whimsically, 'that the Vicomte de Baux used to hurl hostages who couldn't pay their ransom money over this very edge to die a nasty death.'

Philippa peered ghoulishly down to the depths below. 'Did he? I trust he came to a horrible end?'

Amused, Francis replied, 'He did. He drowned in the Rhône trying to escape his pursuers.'

'I'm very pleased to hear it.' Philippa gave another shiver. 'Let's go in. We've seen the sun set, we'll take its rise for granted, shall we?' She raised herself on tiptoes and brushed her lips against his.

Francis held her look for a long moment, his face oddly austere, then he let out a breath and replied, 'Yes, let's. I can think of other warmer, more comfortable places to be.'

'And I've never slept under a canopy before,' said Philippa.

CHAPTER FOUR

FABIEN poured out the Châteauneuf du Pape and exclaimed with quiet satisfaction, 'Well, this is extremely agreeable.'

Sylvie looked at her husband with fond exasperation, caught Philippa's eye across the table and they exchanged a smile.

'Fabien, my sweet, it is much more than that,' Sylvie stated imperially. 'Today is a day to remember!' She eyed Jules and Lisette across the table benignly. 'Who would have thought we would be celebrating an engagement?'

Jules grinned and Lisette gazed adoringly at him. Francis sought Philippa's eye and raised his glass in a silent toast. She returned the gesture, hugging her own personal happiness to her. She was happy, happy, happy, and wanted the world to know, and if not the world, then the friends gathered round the table today.

It was a beautiful late May day. The sun was shining and nature still had a freshness about her despite the warmth of the preceding month. Their table was set on the immaculately trimmed lawn of the hotel where they were dining and their party was the sole occupant, having outstayed the rest of the diners.

'Our ladies are a credit to us,' declared Fabien, his eyes going round the table. 'How beautiful they are. Gentlemen! We are lucky fellows!'

Sylvie, eyes brimming with laughter, broke in, 'I

think we should order coffee now, Fabien. We shall be thrown out if we're not careful.'

'Nonsense,' declared her husband confidently. 'This is a special occasion,' and his smile embraced them all. 'Nevertheless, perhaps we should come down to earth. Coffee would be a good idea, Sylvie.'

The waiter was summoned and coffee ordered. Sylvie, her eyes on Lisette, murmured to Philippa,

'Lisette improves with time, doesn't she?' She shot her friend a sly glance. 'I'm not much good as a matchmaker, am I?' and she gazed reflectively on Francis who was talking to Fabien. She gave a rueful sigh. 'I did so want you to marry a Frenchman so that you'd live in France,' she paused and gave Philippa a teasing look, 'But a half-Frenchman . . .' and she took a sip of wine, her eyes dancing above the rim.

'So you're finishing your holiday on the coast,' Fabien was observing to Francis, the slight hint of a question in his voice.

'We're going to lay a ghost,' admitted Francis quietly. 'Philippa has never been back to Gigaro since her father was killed.'

'Ah, I see. Yes, Sylvie mentioned that. Robert Ingram had an accident, did he not? A fall?'

Francis nodded. 'We're not staying on the coast—the Riviera in June will be crowded. No, we shall stay in the mountains and visit Gigaro from there.' He looked at his watch and turned to Philippa. 'I think we should make a move as soon as we've finished coffee,' and Philippa agreed, glancing back to the hotel and murmuring,

'We've just about overstayed our welcome, I think,' and then her eyes returned to his face.

'Have I told you how beautiful you are

recently?' asked Francis, his voice a lazy caress, the message in his eyes bringing a faint pink to her cheeks.

'Not for at least three hours,' reproached Philippa, her heart singing.

Coffee over, the three couples rose to their feet and amidst much laughter and kissing they departed, each making for their car, calling exuberant farewells. Doors slammed and engines sprang to life, and one by one the cars drew away and went their separate ways.

'Are we mad, do you think?' Philippa asked suddenly, when they had driven in companionable silence for a few miles.

'More than likely,' replied Francis with a drawl, 'and if you keep on looking at me like that I shall have to stop and kiss you. The prospect is not unattractive, but we have a few miles ahead of us.'

'I'll try to behave,' promised Philippa demurely.

La Garde-Freinet, a spacious village dominated by its ruined Saracen castle, lay fourteen kilometres north-west of St Tropez in the mountains known as the Massif des Maures. It was an idyllic setting and Philippa fell in love with it right away. They put up at an inn, small and cosy, with an excellent cuisine, and Philippa, as the days passed, had not thought that such happiness could exist. She kept warning herself that this was not normal living, with the stress and strains of day-to-day problems, but even this sensible attitude did nothing to diminish the magic surrounding them. They made love in the quaint, sloping-ceilinged room, with doves from a nearby cote fluttering and cooing on the roof of the dormer window. Philippa searched for their discarded feathers and made a crown which she presented to Francis with a kiss, saying solemnly,

'Peacocks are in short supply, darling, but here's your crown of feathers,' and she placed it on his head with mock ceremony while Francis took her face in his hands and replied whimsically,

'This troubadour thanks the beautiful lady and swears undying love,' and his mouth covered hers, gently at first, and then whimsy was left behind as their emotions took over, singing their own special poetry.

With three lazy halcyon days behind them they eventually made for Gigaro where the Spider was left parked by an old drinking trough and they took to the cliff path. There was a light breeze off the sea which lifted Philippa's hair, throwing it across her face so that she needed a hand to secure it. Francis tucked her other hand through his arm, still retaining a hold, and they walked without talking. When Philippa slowed to a halt, Francis stared down at the cruel rocks below, frowning, and asked,

'Is this the place?'

She nodded. After a moment, her eyes raking sea and land, she remarked, 'It's very beautiful, isn't it? I'd forgotten how beautiful it is.' She drew him on. 'Let's find the cottage. It's just beyond the next bay, behind those forlorn-looking trees.'

The gate was half off its hinges and the path overgrown. Panes of glass were broken in the windows and weeds were staking a claim across the front door. It was obviously empty.

Philippa turned to Francis who was watching her and explained, 'There's no running water, but the well water is delicious—at least, it was—cold and clear. No electricity or gas.' Her gaze swept

the terrain. 'The whole of this cliff top is covered
in poppies in the summer—it's a fantastic sight.
Splashes of red on green. Dad painted a picture of
me once sitting in the grass surrounded by them
... I wonder where that went to?' She turned back
to the house. 'The door was painted bright poppy
red and—yes, see here? you can just make out
Poppy Cottage on the name-plate.' She contemplated the faded peeling paint and pulled a rueful
face. 'Ah, well, I shall have to remember it the way
it was.'

'Does it distress you?'

Philippa shook her head, leading the way down
the path, placing her feet carefully on the uneven
stones. 'No. I feel sorry for the place, it deserves
better than this, but Poppy Cottage belongs to a
happy childhood and it would be silly to forget
that, wouldn't it?'

Francis took her hand. 'What a sensible person
you are—most of the time,' he added, smiling.

'Stop bragging! It's quite apparent that where
you're concerned I have no sense at all.' Philippa
flicked him a probing look, half laughing, half
serious. 'Do you often make snap decisions,
Francis?'

'What a sweeping question! No, I can't say I
do.' He bent his head and brushed her lips with
his. 'But if I do, there's a good reason.' He pulled
her against him and smiled down into her eyes. 'I
can just see you as a child here—I bet you were a
tomboy, and a bossy-boots.'

Philippa grinned. 'How did you guess?' Her face
sobered and she put her arms round his neck.
'Thank you for helping me to lay the ghosts.' She
glanced back. 'They're friendly ones.' She broke
away and tugged his hand, making him run.

Philippa awoke the next morning early. The sun slanted through the unshuttered window, foretelling another lovely day. She could hear the muted early morning sounds coming from the inn and the doves were awake, their gentle cooing soothing.

She moved her head carefully on the pillow and contentedly lay watching Francis. It was something she liked doing. Their relationship was so new that she was frightened of showing him how much he meant to her. It was a sort of rearguard action which she scorned and yet felt powerless to alter. It still amazed her that they had met at all, let alone fallen in love. So these few moments before he woke were precious ones, for she saw a Francis usually hidden—unaware and defenceless—and she could allow her eyes to wander over him as freely as she liked.

He was lying on his front, his head turned towards her. The arm nearest her was lying heavily across her hip and she was close enough to the rounded curve of his shoulder to put her lips against his skin. She did this, very stealthily, and then ran her tongue over them, tasting him. She could see a smattering of freckles over the sweeping dip to his backbone, bronzed flesh brushed with the fairest of body hair. Her eyes went back to his face. His breathing was quiet. What beautifully shaped lips he had—not full, not thin, but just right, with curved laughter lines faintly visible. His chin was bristly with golden stubble and she resisted the urge to smooth back the front of his hair that was tumbling over his forehead. She wondered lazily how many different colours there were in it and loved the way it sprang, thick and crisp. Her hands itched to press against the, at the moment, untamed thatch of it, but again she resisted the temptation, for that would certainly wake him, and she wanted to hang on to these moments for as long as she could.

Soon, just looking wasn't enough. Fractionally, with great stealth, she eased forward, inching her way so that they touched more completely and her lips curved in anticipation, wondering how long it would be before his body told him and woke him.

She might have known he would take her by surprise. In a single action she was drawn to him by a quick moving arm, his body shifting to accommodate her more thoroughly, and a leg wound itself confidently over her, making her a prisoner. The bristly stubble scrubbed her chin as those beautiful lips claimed hers, first with exuberant enjoyment and then gentling, moving away, wandering down her throat, tasting, exploring with supreme mastery.

Philippa gathered back her breath and demanded, 'How long have you been awake, you wretch?' her colour deepening as his head came up and those incredibly blue eyes enveloped her.

'Long enough,' came the lazy reply. 'I've decided you're a shameful hussy.'

Her lips curved. 'A cat can look at a king ... you'll be late,' she murmured feebly, shivering, as the exquisite drift of his hands travelled sensuously down her back, sliding comfortably over the swell of her hips and coming to rest authoritatively at full stretch, cupping her to him.

She gave in and spread her fingers through his hair and laughed low in her throat, softly. 'I take it,' she managed, her body quivering to the insidious prowess of his tongue, 'that you're not awfully interested in *petit déjeuner*?' and then amusement vanished and she was away on the crest of emotions that left her bereft of any thought that was not coupled with the two of them, in that room, at that moment in time.

Afterwards they lay, their bodies entwined, not saying anything, their breathing gradually returning to normal. The church clock struck the hour.

Francis gave a soft, 'Damn!' and leaned up on one elbow, gazing down at her. He smoothed the hair from her face and said quietly, 'I have to go.'

'Yes, I know.' Philippa lifted a hand and rubbed a finger across the roughness of his chin.

'I'm sorry business has intruded. If I could've put it off I would have done so.' He searched her face and was reassured by her clear gaze.

'The outside world is edging its way in whether we like it or not,' she murmured, giving a small smile.

'But I didn't want it to, not until the holiday was over.'

'Who's being the impractical romantic now?' teased Philippa, her eyes smiling up at him. 'If you hurry you'll have time for coffee.'

'I'll be here for dinner. If anything happens to detain me, I'll ring you.' Francis buried his face in the curve of her neck and shoulder, savouring the moment, before lifting himself off the bed and making for the bathroom.

Philippa listened to the shower running. She knew he had cancelled a number of meetings he had intended to make while in Europe so that they could spend these days together. Now his thoughts would be on what lay ahead, in another world, a world she wasn't part of.

Francis came back, his face already wearing the

look she was beginning to recognise, one of complete absorption in what he was doing. She smiled to herself. Did he realise how he changed and how she was beginning to read him? She watched him get dressed with his usual economy of energy and movement. Here was the Francis emerging she did not know, this stranger in the light grey suit and the purposeful look about him. He could not have risen so highly in the business world without being resourceful and firm. Ruthless? Yes, even ruthless. Francis, on being questioned by her once, had merely said that success was knowing a bit of information at the right time with the right person, but it must be more than that, she mused, her eyes following him as he moved round the room, collecting together his things.

'What will you do while I'm away?' Francis paused to ask, glancing at her before collecting the loose change and car keys from the bedside table.

'I shall work.' Philippa put her hands behind her head and continued mockingly, 'You're not the only one who earns a living. I did have an existence before I met you.'

Francis crossed to the bed and bent down to kiss her, his eyes flickering over her. With his mouth poised above her, he murmured, 'If you don't behave, neither of us will earn a penny piece.' His lips pressed against hers, firmly and briefly. He straightened, saying, 'Take care. I'll see you this evening.' He crossed to the door, hesitated and turned his head her way, his gaze resting pensively on her. 'Pippa . . .'

Philippa sat up and wrapped the sheet round her. 'Go,' she ordered, her voice mock-stern. 'Anything else you have to tell me can wait. You'll be late.'

Francis smiled. 'You sound like a nagging wife! I'm going.'

Philippa looked at the closed door and turned over on to her stomach. How ridiculous she was to feel so forlorn. He was only going to be away a few hours. She had very nearly said drive carefully, which sounded even more wifely! Heaven forbid! She had just stopped herself in time, but she couldn't stop herself thinking it. Was this what love was like then? Worrying? Things must, she thought, get into perspective eventually. She had always been a fatalist, and worrying about Francis driving along the autoroute to Cannes wasn't going to make him drive more carefully, or anyone else, for that matter. There was a bit more to this loving lark than met the eye, that much was evident, she concluded, and drifted into sleep.

Philippa eased her conscience later in the morning by sitting in the sun, adding a few pages to the story she was translating—a children's book from the French into English. At midday she closed her books and returned to their room to lose them in the bottom of her suitcase. Lunch, with an aperitif, beckoned.

A pile of Michelin maps, a couple of magazines and a newspaper had been tidied by the maid and placed on the bedside table. They must have fallen to the floor. Philippa recognised the English paper as the one Francis had bought the day before in St Tropez. He'll be annoyed, she thought, picking it up, remembering him looking for it that morning and murmuring to himself that it must be in the car. She was seized with the sudden urge to find out what was happening in the outside world and took it down with her to read.

She ordered a half-bottle of Pouilly Fuissé and

began to read, enjoying catching up with the news, even though it was already out of date.

There was no reason why she should have read the business pages, except that she had been without a newspaper for so long that now she had one it seemed the thing to do, to digest it from cover to cover. And Francis would have read this section, which was a silly enough reason for reading it, but one that fitted a woman in love. All the incomprehensible information contained in it—stocks and shares, business take-overs, directors kicked out—all would have meant something to Francis.

She nearly missed it. With her interest rapidly dwindling, it was only her own name that caught her eye as she was about to discard the paper. Curious, she began to scan the column.

Shares in Ingrams were gaining strength, owing to an expanding export market. Ingrams, trademark Copperthwaite Wool, were becoming popular abroad—due, no doubt, to the influence of Francis Balfour, one of the directors of Ingrams. Francis Balfour of Balfour Data Products, a firm rising steadily in its own right.

As the chill spread through her, Philippa read on, hoping against hope that it was a mistake. Francis Balfour, the article said, the man who had joined the board of directors five years ago, had expanded interest in the company first of all in France, but interest was growing further afield. Philip Ingram, semi-retired from the company, would make no comment when asked whether his nephew Ross Fairley or Francis Balfour would succeed him as chairman.

Philippa sat, stunned, her whole being weighted down by what she had just learned. Francis

Balfour had just made love to Philip Ingram's granddaughter! The words screamed round in her head, mocking her, tantalising her with a welter of insinuations.

The innkeeper was surprised when Philippa asked him to order her a taxi—surprised, but too polite to show it. Monsieur, he was told, would be arriving back this evening and would settle everything. The car in thirty minutes, please. Madame was charming but firm, and her orders were not to be questioned.

All emotion held firmly in check, Philippa packed quickly and methodically, and when she was done she drew a circle in red pen around the Ingram article and left it lying in the centre of the bed—an ironic place. About to leave, she saw the crown of doves' feathers perched jauntily on the bedpost. She pulled it bitterly to pieces and scattered the feathers over the paper.

The taxi took her to Le Cannet where she hired a Renault and was soon on the autoroute heading west. St Maximin, Aix-en-Provence, Salon, Cavaillon were passed by with Philippa hardly aware of their existence. She knew she needed all the self-control she could summon to do what she had to do, and blocking everything out but the sign to Avignon, she followed the N7 with unswerving concentration.

She paid the toll dues at the Avignon turn-off and made quickly for the car-hire offices where she left the Renault. She went to the bank and cashed a cheque, then took a taxi to Villeneuve. She packed the rest of her belongings, dumped them in the Metro, and returned back across the river, her eyes stonily ignoring the Palace of the Popes, refusing to hear the oh-so-familiar voice declaring that it looked like a fairy cut-out, and not succeeding.

Sylvie, luckily, was in. She opened the door and exclaimed in surprise, 'Phippy! What are you doing here? You're a day early, surely? Is Francis with you?' and peered beyond her friend expectantly, and then took another look at her face. 'Something's wrong, Phippy!' and she drew Philippa with her into the house.

'Sylvie, I haven't much time. Here's the key to the apartment. Will you ask Fabien what I owe him and I'll send a cheque from England.'

'What's the matter? Oh, Phippy dear, what is it?'

'I want to get back home. I've been such a fool—at least, I think I have.'

'You're not making sense.'

'I know—I'm sorry. Francis will come here, looking for me, and I want to get started before he catches up with me.'

Thoroughly alarmed, Sylvie said hurriedly, 'You can't go like this, you'll have an accident! Really, Phippy, you look dreadful. Let me pack you up some food—have you eaten today?'

'Just a croissant and coffee at breakfast.' It seemed easier to give in, and she told Sylvie about the newspaper article while home-made bacon and egg pie, cheese and fruit were hastily packed into a bag. Sylvie listened intently and when Philippa came to an end, she said,

'But why are you running away, Phippy? This isn't like you.'

'I haven't been like myself since meeting Francis, have I?' Philippa came back bitingly.

'Wouldn't it be better to have it out with him? Ask him why he didn't tell you he knew your grandfather?'

'That's what he would prefer. He knows I would find it difficult to believe anything bad about him once he—oh, once he was given the chance to get round me. I need time, Sylvie.'

Sylvie gave a deep sigh. 'It does look bad, but might not the explanation be a simple one?'

'Then why didn't he tell me earlier? He's had so many chances to drop that snippet of information it can't be simple. You said yourself that Grandfather is wealthy. Money and power—two deadly serious things, Sylvie, to some people, and the little I know about Francis is that he doesn't do anything, *anything* on the spur of the moment. Not even falling in love.'

'You don't know that, Phippy,' exclaimed Sylvie miserably. 'None of us have ever seen him like he is with you.'

'Oh, I attract him physically, no doubt about that, which must have been a bonus. Sylvie, I didn't even know his name was Balfour until the Camargue trip—surely that must have been because he wasn't sure how much I knew—whether I was aware that there was a Balfour connected with Copperthwaite?' Philippa gave a distraught laugh. 'God, I went down like a love-starved adolescent right on cue! I took the bait and he hauled me in. Well, I've managed to get off the hook and I have no intention of being eaten alive for dinner.' She stood up and looked wildly around, collecting together her belongings. 'I'm going, Sylvie. I shall cross from Cherbourg, he won't expect me to do that.'

'You think he'll come?'

'He'll come. You might just give him this, and this,' and Philippa struggled with the jewellery Francis had given her over the past few weeks, tossing it down on to the counter top, 'with my compliments.'

Sylvie trailed her worriedly to the door. 'I wish Fabien were here. He'd know what to do,' she observed tearfully, taking Philippa into her arms in a fierce hug.

Philippa managed a good imitation of a laugh. 'You always said I'd be in trouble if ever I fell in love. I wish you hadn't been so right. Damn him! What a gullible fool I've been!' She broke from her friend and stalked down the steps to the Metro.

'Do take care, Phippy,' called Sylvie, 'and ring me. Promise!'

'I will. Sorry to land you in all this.' Philippa backed the car and drove through the gateway, leaving Sylvie standing despondently on the steps, watching her go.

Motorway driving is monotonous and tiring. Philippa intended keeping on the autoroute for as long as she dared, working out the earliest possible time Francis could arrive in Avignon if he returned from Cannes as planned. The Spider was faster than the Metro, but she had some hours' start. Always supposing his plans had not changed—the meeting at Cannes might have finished earlier than expected. Always supposing he came after her. She thought he would. His pride would make him.

It was eight o'clock by the time she reached Lyons and she came off the autoroute and stopped at the first hotel she came to. She left at six o'clock the next morning, driving cross-country to Tours, and then headed north to Cherbourg. She arrived there at seven in the evening, exhausted and numb. She booked a place on the next ferry and managed to get a cabin, then took her place in the car park queue, dozing until a ship's siren told her that the ferry had arrived in from Portsmouth. It would unload its passengers and then she and her fellow travellers could embark. The queue behind her was growing, and all the time she wondered if she would see the Spider come round the corner and nose its way into line. It was an outside chance and she grew cross with herself as her eyes kept flicking nervously to the mirror, but she was not convinced that Francis had not the power to read her mind. She found herself thinking, hurry, hurry! as the cars and lorries disembarked, and had to forcibly make herself relax. It was stupid. If Francis walked up to her now there was nothing she could do about it.

Activity began on the quayside and with a wave of an arm Philippa was directed up the gangplank. She left the Metro in the car bay and made her way to the deck. The ferry was an English-owned vessel and she felt a curious lessening of tension as she heard the crew's voices. She was on a bit of England, or so it seemed, and nearly home.

For three-quarters of an hour she stood by the rail, the darkness closing in around her, and when there had been no vehicle arrive for a third of that time, she began to feel she could relax. She was joined at the rail by a woman passenger, and Philippa, out of politeness, made conversation. During their talk they found they were sharing the same cabin.

When the white Alfa Romeo came slowly round the corner, the lights from the quay picking out the number plate, Philippa hardly noticed it, and then, as it came nearer, it registered. She must have made some exclamation, because the woman looked at her, then turned her attention down to the car.

'Someone you know?' she asked, and Philippa nodded, feeling sick with disappointment. Making her excuses, she went to find the cabin.

She sat on the bunk, her head in her hands. She had felt all the time that she was not going to make it. The whys and wherefores did not matter. What did was that Francis would be on the ship and he would try and contact her.

The door opened and the woman from the deck came in. She looked at the two sets of double bunks and settled herself on the bottom of the other one.

'The purser reckons there'll be just us in here. Some people don't think the crossing's long enough to warrant a berth, but if there's one going I always take it. I'm Joan, by the way, Joan Markham.'

Philippa returned her own name. It was a relief, in a way, to have to make talk. It stopped her thinking about Francis. Mrs Markham, her husband and son had been camping, so she told Philippa, in Brittany. After a while, Mrs Markham said,

'You look tired. Better get some sleep.'

Philippa nodded. She ached with fatigue and her head was beginning to pound.

'Is your car a red Metro?' Mrs Markham asked casually, and startled, Philippa said,

'Yes—how did you know?'

'Are you in trouble? I don't want to pry, but I've a daughter of my own and if she was in difficulty I wouldn't like to think no one would help her.'

'You're very kind,' began Philippa helplessly, and then, 'Not in trouble, exactly.'

'Something to do with the white Italian car, isn't it? You went so pale when you saw it I thought you were going to faint. Is he following you, the driver?'

'Yes.' Philippa felt too ill to prevaricate and it was obvious her companion knew something. What did it matter anyway? Francis had caught up with her, and she so wanted a breathing space, time to distance herself from him and find a sense of proportion again. At the moment she couldn't even think straight.

'I waited for him to come up,' Mrs Markham was saying, 'not intentionally, you understand, I was looking for Jimmy, my son—fourteen and an absolute terror for disappearing when you want him. I went to look for him in the car bay, knowing how crazy he is about engines, and the engine room leads off from the bay, you see. He was there, right enough, chatting to some of the crew. I saw the white car being directed into line and the driver got out—a good-looking fellow, with fair hair. I thought he'd come up the steps, but he didn't, he wandered down the rows of cars until he came to the red Metro. Then he came up. Passed me with a nice smile, though his face had been a bit grim.' She paused. 'Nothing is as bad as it seems, my dear. Have you had a tiff?'

Philippa was lost in thought. She swung round and gave the other woman all her attention, saying urgently, 'Does your Jimmy know about tyres? Enough to let one down?'

Mrs Markham laughed, 'I shouldn't be at all surprised!' The ship shuddered and the engine noise increased. 'We're away.'

Her story had to be good enough to warrant action on Jimmy's part, Philippa decided, her mind racing. She had always had a good imagination. 'The fair man ... he's ... my husband, and I came home earlier than expected—we live in France, he's half-French—and found him with someone else. I ... I caught them together, you see.' Would this explanation do? Mrs Markham gave a sympathetic murmur, and encouraged, Philippa went on, 'I just turned tail and ran. I thought he'd miss the boat, but as you saw, he didn't. I want to have a breathing space to think things over. If Jimmy could let down a tyre for me I'd have the chance to give him the slip.'

'Men! Just wait here—I'll have a word with Jimmy. You wouldn't like more than one tyre?'

Philippa choked a laugh and shook her head. 'Just one will do. Tell Jimmy to be careful, I shouldn't like him to get into trouble, and,' she got out her purse, 'give him this and tell him to treat himself.'

'Bribery and corruption work wonders,' agreed Jimmy's mother, and she took the money and went out. Twenty minutes later she was back. 'It's done. Don't worry, my dear, you'll be off and away when we arrive at Portsmouth. Now try and get some sleep. I'll do the same,' and she lay down on the bunk opposite and gave a chuckle. 'Quite an experience for Jimmy, being encouraged to commit a crime! It'll take some getting over.'

To her surprise, Philippa slept deeply. The shuddering of the engines in reverse woke her. Sitting up quickly, she opened her eyes and decided she felt awful, lying back with a groan. Her berth companion entered, carrying a cup.

'I've brought you this. I took the chance you were a coffee drinker.' She handed over the cup, sitting down herself to give the younger girl a thoughtful look. 'Your husband's in the restaurant, brooding over his.'

Philippa's hand jerked, nearly spilling the coffee. It was a shock to hear Francis called her husband.

'Now you listen to me, my dear. Think hard about what you're going to do. You've got to stop running some time and when you do, make sure you know what you really want. Maybe you'll see things differently in a day or two, but don't do anything in a rush. I'm not condoning your husband, but men don't see such things quite the same way as women do. If you love him, think what it will be like without him, eh?'

Philippa gave a wan smile. 'It's a bit more complicated than that, Mrs Markham.'

'Maybe, but most things come down to the basics in the end. And you be careful—he doesn't look the sort to cross.' Mrs Markham stood up and collected her things. 'Take care now,' and with an encouraging smile she left.

Philippa bestirred herself and went to the washroom. Feeling a little better, she gathered together her belongings just as the tannoy issued its orders for car passengers to go to their cars.

The passageway was crowded with people and she eased her way into the general exodus. Some yards along her wrist was grasped strongly and she was pulled urgently out of the queue, the well-known drawling voice saying, 'Sorry—excuse me—thanks,' to those who had to give way, which they did with no interest in the fair man with the set, resolute face and cold blue eyes or the girl who allowed it to happen because she did not want to cause an embarrassing scene.

'Let me go, Francis,' said Philippa, when she was clear, not raising her voice, but glaring at him with angry eyes. She pulled ineffectually at his grasp, which did not lessen.

'Pippa, we must talk.'

'Don't you dare call me that—don't you *ever* dare to call me that again!' She wrenched her wrist once more. '*Will* you please let me go—I can't bear you to touch me!' She ground the words out with deep loathing.

'Won't you let me explain?'

Philippa gave a bitter laugh. 'Oh, I'm sure you could sweet-talk your way into some semblance of explanation.' She took a deep breath. 'I loathe and despise you, and I never want to see you again!'

Remote, the pale patrician face as expressionless as marble, Francis relaxed his grip and released her. Eyes hooded, a small tight smile appeared on his lips and he drawled, 'Forgive me for delaying you,' and stepped aside with obnoxious politeness.

A crewman coaxing along a few remaining stragglers called, 'Everyone to their cars. Hurry along, please!'

Rubbing her wrist, Philippa resisted the temptation to strike that cold smile from Francis' face, and swinging away, she stalked after the crewman. Francis let her go.

In the car bay the noise of the car engines, the exhaust fumes and the lorries revving battered Philippa's senses. She flung herself into the Metro and started it, glaring stonily ahead.

Damn him—damn him! She was unaware of the tears streaming down her face as she followed the lorries up the ramp and off the ferry. She was waved through Customs without being stopped and headed for London.

She imagined the scene she was leaving

behind—all the cars leaving and Francis pumping up the flat tyre.

Serve him right!

It did not help knowing that if he had said, I love you, she would have gone into his arms.

With gritted teeth and knuckles white on the steering wheel, Philippa told herself grimly, 'Then it's a good job he didn't say it, isn't it?'

CHAPTER FIVE

'You have had a busy holiday, haven't you, darling?' said Grace Stanhope to her niece. She was sitting behind her desk, glasses removed, books piled high all round, a half-filled sheet of typing, an article she was writing for a magazine, set before her in the typewriter. She put a finger in the open page of one of the books to keep the place and waited patiently. She did not allow any of the surprise she felt at the news just imparted to show on her face or appear in her voice.

Grace's matter-of-fact understatement, so typical of her attitude to life in general, was a welcome relief to Philippa's own twisted, shredded emotions. Even the telling seemed to help, and she gave a reluctant laugh and said wryly,

'You can't be thinking me any bigger a fool than I think myself.'

'Falling in love isn't foolish. It's how it can cloud one's judgment, even making the simplest of decisions. For instance, you didn't consider waiting to ask him for an explanation, this Francis of yours?'

'I did think about it, yes,' replied Philippa a little defensively, 'but I knew if I let him . . . that he would . . .'

'Persuade you by soft voice and gentle touch— now who said that?—no matter. I quite understand what you're trying to say. I'm not in my dotage yet.'

'Yes, well, I wasn't thinking too much of explanations. It was not telling me he knew the

Ingrams, was involved in the family business, that was such a shock, such a hurt. How could he have not told me that? There must be a reason.'

'Perhaps he intended to eventually and left it too late.'

'There's nothing indecisive about Francis, Grace. You'd know that if you met him. It was sheer bad luck for him that I read that newspaper. No, he has too much control over his life—and why are you making excuses for him? Whose side are you on anyway?'

Grace raised her brows at the outburst. 'You know I like to see every point of view—and he doesn't appear to have controlled things too well at the moment, does he?'

'He hasn't done too badly,' muttered Philippa grimly.

'What are you going to do now?'

'Catch up on work and forget him.'

'Be sensible, darling!'

Philippa gave an impatient laugh. 'Oh, very well—short term, I shall work, long term, I shall go to Cumbria and introduce myself to my grandfather.'

Approval showed on her aunt's face. 'I think that's a good idea. When will you go?'

'I'll wait for the birthday celebration in September.'

'And if your Francis comes here?'

'I shan't see him.' It came out defiantly, but as her aunt's countenance did not alter from one of calm interest, Philippa said less aggressively, 'I don't think he'll come, Grace, but if he does, or if he phones, I shan't speak to him. My guess is that he'll wait until September, because I'm positive he'll be there, at Grandfather's.'

'He sounds an extraordinary young man. There can't be many who could have such patience.'

'Francis has,' retorted Philippa, remembering acutely the delicate patience of his wooing.

'I look forward to meeting him,' Grace acknowledged. 'Any man who can sweep you off your feet must be special.' Her eye caught a word on the open page. 'Ah, just the word I was looking for.' She looked up, satisfied, and carried on. 'I was beginning to think you were too much like me.'

Philippa smiled reluctantly. 'What's that supposed to mean?'

'It means, my dear Philippa, that I like my own way too much. I've been on the verge of saying "yes" to marriage a couple of times in my forty-odd years, and each time the thought of spending the rest of my life having to consider another person before I can do what I want to do held me back. However, what suits me doesn't suit everyone, and I suspected not you. I'm glad to hear I'm right. I must remember to thank your Francis.'

'I can't see anything to be glad about,' muttered Philippa crossly, 'and I wish you wouldn't keep on calling him *my* Francis.'

Ignoring the exasperated interruption, Grace went on, 'I've never said this to you before, Philippa, but I strongly disagreed with Robert keeping you away from the Ingrams.'

Philippa stared, indignation rising. 'They didn't want to know us! My precious grandfather didn't even send an acknowledgment when Mother died! I know he was told, because I wrote to him!'

Startled, Grace echoed, 'You wrote?'

'Yes, I sent him a letter. He didn't answer it.'

'But, my dear, you were only...' Grace frowned, working it out, '... eight at the time. Did Robert know?'

'No. I did it all by myself, except for addressing the envelope. I got one of the barmen to do that, and I posted it myself.'

There was silence while Grace digested this piece of news. She said at last, 'I'm not saying your grandfather was right in all this, Philippa, I'm merely looking at it with regard to yourself. Robert should have made some attempt to heal the breach, but he only lived for the present. If he had money to buy canvas and paint...'

'He loved me. He looked after me.'

'Darling, of course he did, but if he'd been a different type of man he would have considered your future. It isn't right to wipe out half of one's family. Who have you, beside me?'

'I've never needed anyone other than you. I didn't know you felt like this. You've never said.' Philippa looked at her aunt, puzzled.

'The question didn't arise. Now it has. You should go to Cumbria, meet your family, and make up your own mind about them. I realise that it's already made up, in one respect. No one likes to be ignored for twenty-seven years, but now you have an invitation to visit.'

Philippa considered her aunt thoughtfully. Grace had never been one to thrust her opinions on anyone. She was there when needed, but was not obtrusive. Philippa knew she owed a lot to Grace's sensible view of life. She said slowly,

'You told me once that I was my grandfather's heir.'

Grace lifted her head from her books. 'Yes, that's right.'

'I suspect that's why Francis . . .' Philippa broke off, a mixture of bitterness and anger welling up.

'Darling, that's a bit Gothic, isn't it? And not very subtle—making up to the heir in the hopes of a fat legacy! Your grandfather does have other relations.'

'Exactly! I don't want his wretched money!'

Grace ignored this outburst and went on musingly, 'There's your father's older sister— that's your aunt Harriet, she must be in her early sixties and to my knowledge has never married. The other brother was drowned as a child, so yes, you must be the direct heir.'

'I've been thinking a lot about them, just lately—Mum and Dad, I mean,' Philippa smiled. 'Not many people can boast that their parents ran away to get married.'

Grace gave an impatient snort. 'They were a couple of romantics, both of them. Infants! Rose would have lived anywhere with Robert and because Robert was happy, Rose was.'

'Did you like him?' asked Philippa suddenly.

'Who, Robert?' Grace smiled. 'Of course I liked him—he was an extremely likeable person. I didn't always approve of him, but he made Rose happy and he loved you, when he remembered you.' She paused and went on musingly, 'I've always wondered why he never married again after Rose died. He didn't seem the sort to live alone.'

Philippa grinned. 'He didn't, there was always his latest model. They were nice women, and kind to me. Besotted with Father, every last one of them, and he was always so offhand, but I suppose that was part of his charm.'

'He did have charm, Robert, and he was selfish, as all true artists are.' Grace shut her books with a bang. 'Let's go and eat. I pushed a chicken in the oven when you rang and it should be cooked by now.' She rose. 'If Francis Balfour comes knocking at my door I ought to be able to recognise him. Describe him to me, Philippa.'

Her niece rubbed a finger across her forehead. For a few minutes she had forgotten Francis, but he was not going to be wiped out that easily. 'He's about six foot, slim, fair and blue-eyed.' She stopped and gave an impatient sigh. 'Wait, I have a photograph of him somewhere,' and she rummaged in her bag and took from it a snapshot which she handed to Grace. She waited, almost nervously, for comment, remembering the day she had taken it, and the zany, mad mood they were in.

Grace studied it for a moment and observed drily, 'I can quite see why you fell, darling, and you say he has brains as well? What a bonus! I doubt he'll let you go without a struggle, there's a possessive look in those eyes of his.' She handed the photograph back. 'I don't need to tell you not to cut off your nose to spite your face, do I?'

'I suppose you think I'm being silly.'

'No, no—you're feeling vulnerable ... love's like that, and you want to find out if your Francis loves you or Philip Ingram's granddaughter. Come along, let's eat. And then you'd better go to bed. Making a fool of oneself can be very tiring.'

Grace's astringency was like a tonic. Philippa found herself laughing and followed her aunt into the kitchen, smelt the chicken casserole and found she was hungry.

Philippa settled into everyday living. At first, each time the telephone or doorbell rang she tensed before answering. Then, as Francis made no move to contact her, she was afflicted with a mass of contradictory feelings, depending on her mood of the moment. Unhappiness lay like a heavy weight inside her and she was beset with doubts and fears. Had she been too hard—too condemning? These were brushed aside by flashes of anger. She came to accept the moodiness fairly philosophically. She had told Francis on the ferry that she did not want to see him again and he had accepted that—which was an admission of guilt if ever there was one! She was left with her pride and her work, neither good bedfellows. She was learning that the clock could not be put back. Those golden days in Provence could never be recaptured, but the memories clung like a limpet. She was a different person because of them. Not completely whole, as yet, but time, so they said, was a great healer.

Work took her to Brussels and Geneva. She finished the children's stories and started on a travel book on Italy. One day she returned home to find that a huge basket of poppies had been delivered. Grace had taken them in, questioned the delivery girl, who knew nothing of the order.

Seeing the splash of colour, the fragile petals, Philippa was immediately transported to the cliff top with the breeze blowing off the Mediterranean and Francis standing with her close to him as she told him about the poppies that grew there in the summer months. She shut the image from her mind. It still hurt like hell. There was no message on the card, but none was necessary.

Grace said, 'They don't last, poppies, once they've been cut.'

'How symbolic,' replied Philippa stiffly, and Grace made no further comment, only making a mild request for their removal because of her hay fever. Philippa could not bring herself to throw them away and took them to an old people's home nearby, after taking one perfectly formed bloom and pressing it between two books. It would be a sardonic reminder not to be such a fool again.

The telephone rang one evening mid-week and it was not until a stranger's voice answered that Philippa realised how much she had wanted it to be Francis. She would, naturally, have put the phone down, but . . .

'Philippa Ingram?' The man's voice was pleasant and warm. 'My name is Ross Fairley. That probably means nothing to you, but we're cousins.'

'Are we?' replied Philippa cautiously, adding, 'How nice of you to call.'

He must have picked up a nuance of uncertainty in her voice, for he laughed and said, 'Look, we really are related. Your grandfather, Philip Ingram, is my great-uncle. My grandmother was his sister. Now, that's not too confusing, is it?' His voice had a smile in it, a teasing quality that Philippa found disarming, and she laughed.

'I think I can about grasp that.'

'Good. We're all delighted to learn that you're coming to Uncle's birthday celebrations, and as my sister Lucy and I are in London at the moment we wondered if you'd like to meet up with us and we can introduce ourselves so that when you finally come to Copperthwaite you'll at least know us.'

Touched by this consideration, Philippa exclaimed, 'Why, thank you, I'd like that. When do you suggest?'

'Tomorrow evening? Is that too short notice?'

Philippa hastily glanced at her engagement pad and answered, 'Yes, that's fine.'

'Excellent—I'll pick you up, say, around eight?'

Ross Fairley turned out to be in his early thirties, with light brown hair, grey eyes and pleasant features. Smiling, he took Philippa's hand in his and said warmly,

'So! I meet the long-lost granddaughter at last!'

'I haven't really been lost,' replied Philippa wryly, and his smile turned downwards as he responded quickly,

'No, of course you haven't—I'm sorry, that was a thoughtless remark, but my pleasure at meeting you is genuine, I assure you. Lucy and I have wondered about you for years.' He studied her face, his own serious. 'I do hope you can forgive Uncle Philip. He's an old man now and . . .' He ran fingers through his hair and gave a likeable grimace coupled with an expressive shrug of the shoulders. 'You're coming to Copperthwaite and that's all that matters.'

Feeling sorry for the awkwardness, Philippa smiled and said, 'I'm looking forward to it, but have to admit I'm a bit nervous. Meeting you and your sister tonight will be a great help.' She peered beyond him. 'Isn't Lucy with you?'

'No.' Ross followed her into the hallway. 'She'll be at the restaurant waiting for us—I hope!' He grinned. 'Lucy is notorious for being late, but I read her the riot act before I left. You're obviously not like her—a punctual lady is a bonus I hadn't expected!'

Philippa had not expected his words to trigger off the memory of Francis saying almost the same thing. These spasmodic yet nerve-racking memories came like blinding flashes out of nowhere and as usual left her feeling shaken.

As they drove into the centre of the city Ross, in an obvious endeavour to put her at her ease, talked.

'Did you know that Lucy and I live at Copperthwaite?' His side-glance took in Philippa's negative shake of the head. 'The reason is that we're orphans, our parents were killed when I was six and Lucy only a baby. They were experienced climbers, so I've been told, who went to another climber's aid during appalling, unexpected weather conditions on a weekend climb in Scotland. To be truthful I can barely remember them and Lucy not at all. Great-Uncle took us in and made himself responsible for us, and Harriet—that's your Aunt Harriet—helped bring us up. I work at the Copperthwaite Mills and call your grandfather Uncle Philip outside their walls and Sir inside them. Lucy calls him Nunkie, but she can get away with anything.'

'How old is Lucy?' asked Philippa, and he smiled indulgently.

'She's twenty-five, beautiful and terribly spoiled. She has a share in a Keswick boutique. I'm thirty, intelligent, kind to animals and the elderly, and like taking extremely attractive new cousins out for dinner.'

Ross's lighthearted conversation was pleasant and Philippa's spirits lifted. If Lucy was as nice as her brother then Copperthwaite wouldn't be so daunting. She drew her jacket round her shoulders while she waited for Ross to park the car and they walked the rest of the way to the restaurant, arms linked, finding out that they both loved London and exchanging favourite places.

Subdued lights, a bustle of waiters serving food and an agreeable murmur of conversation greeted

them as they entered the restaurant. The manager
glided forward and accepted Ross's name with a
welcoming smile. A flick of the fingers brought the
head waiter to their side and he led the way down
the room to their table. Ross turned a grinning
face over his shoulder to exclaim, 'Wonders will
never cease—Lucy's here before us!'

The table was blocked from view, but as the
waiter stepped aside Ross drew Philippa forward
eagerly, introducing her with much enthusiasm to
his sister.

Lucy was indeed a very lovely girl, with a clear
pale skin and fine straight hair, parted in the
middle, which fell way beyond her shoulders, the
almost white blondeness a startling contrast to the
ruby red dress she was wearing. She had her
brother's grey eyes but not his spontaneous
friendliness. There was a slightly bored, indolent
air about her that Philippa suspected covered up a
wariness, maybe a resentment over this meeting.
After all, if Lucy Fairley had been living at
Copperthwaite all her life, why should she
welcome Philippa with open arms?

Ross was now saying, as he took a step
sideways, 'We hope you don't mind, Philippa, but
to even up the numbers we've invited an old friend
of ours to join us.'

Philippa found she was staring straight into the
cool, offensively amused blue eyes of Francis, and
she was unable to conceal the sharp intake of
breath as she drowned helplessly in their depths.

The smile that had automatically been forming
on her lips froze. Her hand was taken in his and
she found herself saying, 'How do you do?' and he
was saying, 'I've been looking forward to this
meeting,' which unleashed the flood of anger

within her and her eyes flashed the reply—I bet
you have!

With great politeness Francis pulled out a chair
for her and she sat down. As Lucy and Ross
exchanged words she turned to him and demanded
in a furious undertone,

'What the hell are you doing here?'

'Like the proverbial bad penny, you'll find that I
always turn up,' he replied, matching his tone to
hers, and then, 'What do you fancy to eat?'

'My appetite has strangely disappeared. What
I'd really like to do is get up and walk out, but you
know damn well I can't do that.'

'It would provoke some awkward questions,'
agreed Francis smoothly, his eyes on the menu,
'which you evidently are not prepared to answer.'
He turned his head, one brow raised, eyes
challenging.

'You're right, I'm not,' replied Philippa em-
phatically, returning his look with equal intent and
then regarding the menu, although it could have
been in Chinese for all she could take the words in.

When their orders had been given Lucy
monopolised the conversation for a while, talking
about a fashion exhibition she had been to see,
also dropping in the fact that she and Francis had
been to see a West End hit musical the night
before together.

Philippa smiled, and conversed, and ate her
food, which was tasteless ... and tried to stop
herself hating Lucy. It was difficult to ignore the
fact that Lucy and Francis had known each other
for some years, and the thought came whirling
into her head that they had been lovers. At this
idea a wave of jealousy swept through her, its
intensity leaving her feeling sick. If you don't want

him, it can't matter, can it? she told herself angrily,
and hardened her resolve to armour herself against
any more hurt. She knew now that her instinct to
keep right out of his way had been sound. He still
had the power, if she let him, to reduce her to a
senseless idiot.

In any other circumstances this meeting with her
new cousins would have been highly enjoyable, but
even if she disregarded Francis sitting next to her,
she couldn't blot him out completely. She thought
he looked singularly well—when he should have
been looking haggard and drawn. As always he
seemed to outshine every man in the room, and he
certainly made a great effort to keep the evening
rolling along, she would grant him that. She only
hoped her own performance was as good.

She might have known he would engineer things
to his advantage. Before she was aware of what
was happening it was decided that Francis was
taking her home. It seemed logical that brother
and sister should return together to their hotel,
and although Philippa began to make some
babbling attempt to say she could take a taxi, this
was naturally overruled. As Ross and Lucy bade
her goodbye with the promise of her visit to
Cumbria ahead, Philippa found herself walking
towards the Spider, parked in a side street,
Francis' hand firmly beneath her elbow. As they
turned the corner, out of sight of the Fairleys, she
whirled round, wrenching her arm away, saying
vehemently,

'I thought I told you I didn't want to see you
again!'

Francis bent to unlock the door and opened it.
He said calmly, 'I know what you said, Philippa,
but even you have to admit the request is

unreasonable and unrealistic. Get in and I'll take you home ... or aren't you strong enough to be alone in my company for the time that takes?' He watched her with bleak amusement as she struggled with the implications of that taunt. Philippa knew there was too much truth involved for her not to pick up the challenge.

Without another word she slid into the car and Francis closed the door, his countenance quite impassive, carefully not allowing any hint of satisfaction to show. In a few moments they were drawing away and Philippa said, 'Where are you taking me?'

Francis rattled off her address, adding, 'That's where you want to go, isn't it? If not, I'm more than willing to take you back to my flat.' His voice was insufferably expressionless.

Philippa threw him a cold look and they spoke no more until they neared Wimbledon, when Francis asked for more detailed directions which Philippa gave as briefly as possible. As the Spider slowed to a halt she said swiftly,

'Thank you for the lift,' and made a move to leave. Francis' hand clamped down on her wrist, fingers and thumb encircling with a grip that brooked no nonsense. Philippa's head swung round and with her chin up she sustained his long, steady look.

'You're not going to get rid of me easily, Pippa,' he said softly. She answered numbly, 'Thanks for the warning,' and looked pointedly down at her wrist.

Francis lifted the wrist and placed his lips gently on the jumping pulse, and a small tremor went through her. Mutely, he let her go, widening his fingers to allow her to pull away.

As she walked up the path to the front door she knew he was watching her gain entry. When she stepped inside she heard the Spider accelerate off.

How dared he waltz back into her life with such brazen coolness! And no word of explanation! Philippa glared at her reflection in the mirror as she cleaned her teeth. Would you have listened? she asked herself, and scowled. She went to bed, tossed and turned, and wondered how someone so organised and sensible as herself could land in such a quagmire.

In late August she received a letter from her aunt Harriet.

'They would like me to go up the week before Grandfather's birthday,' she told Grace. She read the address at the top of the page and murmured, 'Copperthwaite, Caldbeck, Cumbria—it has a lovely sound to it, doesn't it?'

Grace said, 'Cumbria has Norse origins. Thwaite, I think, is a clearing in a forest. Will you go earlier?'

'One part of me thinks yes, the other holds back,' admitted Philippa. 'I think I must still have my childhood hang-up about the Ingrams. I really worked up a hatred of them, Grace ... blew them up out of all proportion, of course. I do realise nothing can be totally one-sided and Father must have hurt them too.'

'Well, you've already met your Fairley cousins, so that's a help, but going up earlier would mean meeting the rest by degrees, instead of having the whole lot thrust on you in one go. Your presence is bound to create an interest, isn't it?'

'Long-lost granddaughter,' Philippa added wryly, and Grace gave a philosophic shrug.

Philippa had told her aunt about her meal out
with the Fairleys, and that Francis had been
present also—just the bare details, and Grace had
not questioned her further.

'It's a pleasant letter,' Grace said, and Philippa
nodded. Her aunt Harriet sounded nice and she
remembered her father speaking of her with
affection.

'I think I shall go earlier,' she decided suddenly. 'I
think I can organise my work around those dates.'

As motorways go, the M6 was surprisingly
attractive. The distance from London to Penrith
was not far short of three hundred miles and the
last seventy before Penrith were truly beautiful.
Philippa hardly knew what to expect, but the
distant peaks excited her and seemed to draw her
on. She came off the motorway at junction 40 and
took the Keswick road, turning north for
Caldbeck and following the National Park
boundary all the way.

Caldbeck looked a real working village, not yet
taken over completely by the tourist trade. It had a
traditional village green, a duckpond, a twelfth-
century church and the fame of John Peel, the
huntsman with the grey coat and the hounds, lying
buried in the churchyard.

Philippa parked the car and found a café where
she ordered a pot of tea and took out the latest
letter from her aunt which enclosed a pencil
drawing of the route to Copperthwaite from
Caldbeck. The letter was short but welcoming.
Philippa thought her aunt Harriet might be an
ally—for she had to admit that she could find no
filial feelings for Philip Ingram, her grandfather,
only strong curiosity.

Deciding she was only putting off the evil hour, Philippa drank up and made herself clean and tidy in the ladies' room, paid her bill and strolled back to the car. It was a pleasant day, but she was glad of the trouser suit she was wearing, for the breeze was fresh. She spread out the Ordnance Survey map across the passenger seat and took stock. Her eyes picked up names like Willy Knott, High Pike and Little Cockup, teasing her interest in the land of her forebears. Aunt Harriet had suggested she brought stout walking shoes with her, for the best way to see Cumbria was on foot. Philippa liked walking and was happy to do as her aunt suggested, and the map whetted her appetite.

Memorising the route which took her off the main road, she drove out of Caldbeck and a mile or so out of the village came to the turn-off and crossed the cattle grid. The road now wound over the fells, unfenced, crossing a small bridge straddling a quick-flowing beck. The sign Philippa was looking for, to Copperthwaite, directed her along a road to the right which, although having a good surface, was narrow and bordered either side with a ditch. For a while the road climbed, and then she saw Copperthwaite for the first time. The house was in a dip and rose starkly out of the landscape. Not by any stretch of the imagination could Copperthwaite be called beautiful, although there was, perhaps, a kind of beauty in the weathered brickwork matching the starkness of the fells rising above it, making the house impressive, even imposing in a solid way.

Philippa wondered what it would be like in winter, for the winds would sweep across the fells from the sea and there was very little protection for the house. A line of copper beeches was standing tall along the west boundary and hedges and bushes formed some kind of perimeter along the three other sides. There was a well kept kitchen garden in the southern corner and a few ornamental tubs with brightly coloured annuals still showing bravely. The fells seemed to come right up to the house.

Philippa drew up before the front and switched off the engine. She sat for a moment, unwilling to make a move, when a figure appeared at the door. A woman hurried down the stone steps and crunched across the gravel.

'Philippa? Yes, I thought it must be you. How lovely! Have you had a good journey? You must be tired, such a long way for you to drive—but then you modern girls do everything, don't you? Lucy tells me I'm sadly out of date, and she's right, of course. Will you put the car round by the side of the house, dear? I'll send someone for your luggage . . .'

'Oh, no, that won't be necessary, I can carry it. Er—it is Aunt Harriet, isn't it?'

Her aunt gave a laugh. 'Yes, how silly of me!' Her hands fluttered in the way Philippa was to recognise as a gesture peculiarly her own, and she embraced her niece, murmuring, 'It's been too long. Really, Robert was very naughty, but you've come at last and we shall get to know you. I shall go and tell Father you've arrived. You shall see him at dinner.'

Philippa found she was smiling as she parked the Metro. Her aunt's absentminded air was belied by the straightforward instructions in her letters. She could not see anything of her father in Harriet—brother and sister were not alike physically. Harriet had grey eyes, Robert's had been brown, and Harriet was tiny and dumpy whereas Robert had been tall and thin, but there was something in the smile that was reminiscent of her father, Philippa thought, as she dragged the case from the rear of the car.

'Can I take that for you, Miss Philippa?'

Philippa turned and saw a man coming towards her, dressed in a dark suit, the jacket of which he was still putting on, as if he had been disturbed.

'Thank you,' replied Philippa, smiling, 'although it's not heavy.'

He returned the smile. He looked to be in his early forties, strongly built and with the soft burr of the south-west county accent.

'I'm Ainsley, miss—I look after your grandfather.' As he said this he began to walk towards the house, and Philippa followed, asking,

'How is my grandfather?'

'As well as can be expected. He's been looking forward to your coming.'

They had now entered the house and were climbing the stairs, a long landing leading off. They passed three doors and the fourth Ainsley opened, indicating Philippa to precede him.

'This is your room, miss.' He put the case on a chair just inside the door. 'Dinner's at seven, and it's a formal affair—Mr Ingram likes to keep the old customs. There's hot water in the bathroom two doors further on, and if you go to the end there,' he pointed along the landing, 'you'll find the main stairs. The drawing-room's on the left, the dining-room on the right.' He gave the room a quick appraisal and then said quietly, 'Welcome home, Miss Philippa. If you need anything, just ask,' and then he was walking briskly back down the landing.

Welcome home! Thoughtfully Philippa closed the door.

She crossed to the window. The room faced north with a sweeping view of the fells. They were in sunshine at the moment, soft greens and browns, but as the clouds passed briefly over the sun there was an indication of a much harsher picture, although one still demanding admiration. She stood, frowning pensively. Somehow she just could not imagine her father living out his life in this rugged part of the world. He fitted in much better in the hot, easygoing atmosphere of southern France.

A pang of homesickness tinged with panic swept over her. She was back in Provence with the sun burning her skin and Francis was smoothing oil over her body as they lay on the rocks of a small bay, made private by a particularly steep descent to which only the nimble and determined applied themselves. She could feel his hands still, as they worked their way along her arms and shoulders and down her back, and a wave of physical longing to be able to turn the clock back enveloped her with such intensity that she felt dizzy. Taking a deep breath, she turned from the window and made herself concentrate on the room. The walls were papered in a delicate rosebud pattern and the curtains and carpet echoed the deep rose pink. The furniture was old and well cared for and the whole was pleasing to the eye.

Philippa bathed and dressed for dinner, choosing a black dress which she considered would see her through the first meeting with her grandfather. It had long sleeves and was draped from one shoulder and caught in at the waist, the folds

following through the line of the skirt. She took
particular care with her face—she looked rather
pale, but that was probably nerves—and her hair,
and with nothing more to keep her she ventured
out and sought the main stairs. When she was
halfway down, the door on the left of the hall
opened and Ross came striding out, pausing on
seeing her.

'Hello, Philippa! You've arrived safely, I see. I
was just coming to find you.' He held out
welcoming hands and Philippa ran down the
remaining stairs and returned his smile.

'Oh, Ross, you can't imagine how good it is to
see a face I know!' she exclaimed, laughing
ruefully.

'Are you nervous? No need to be.' He looked at
her admiringly. 'Uncle's had a couple of bad days,
but he's a little better today and you'll do his old
heart good when he sees you—you're an Ingram
right enough. As you see,' and he indicated his
evening suit, 'your grandfather is a stickler for the
old rules. Come along and let me get you a drink,
you probably need one. What would you like?' He
stood aside as he opened the door and as Philippa
entered the room she was relieved to find her
grandfather was not present. Lucy was sprawled in
graceful ease in a nearby armchair, turning the
pages of a magazine in a desultory manner, and
Harriet was sitting on a sofa. Both greeted
Philippa, Lucy with a half-wave of the hand and
Harriet with a beaming smile, and as Philippa
murmured, 'Sherry, please,' to Ross's question, he
went to pour out the drink.

'What do you think of Copperthwaite, now
you're here?' he asked, as he handed her the
glass.

'It's much bigger than I expected,' admitted Philippa, adding, 'Where are the Copperthwaite Mills?'

Lucy looked up in surprise. 'Goodness, you really don't know anything, do you? They're in Carlisle.'

'We scan four generations,' Harriet added, 'and the Copperthwaite Wool Mark is known the whole world over.' She glanced at the carriage clock on the mantel and frowned. 'I think we'd better go in, children. Father is such a stickler for punctuality at mealtimes.'

Lucy tossed down the magazine and rose, walking languidly to the door. She was looking lovely in a cream silk-knit dress and made no effort to include Philippa as they crossed the hall to the dining-room.

'Chin up,' whispered Ross, his eyes signalling encouragement. 'Uncle's bark is worse than his bite!'

'Good evening, Father,' said Harriet, a little flustered. 'Here is Philippa.'

'So I see.' Philip Ingram nodded at Ross, lifted his cheek for Lucy to kiss, his eyes all the time upon Philippa, who was thinking with shocked surprise—why, he's in a wheelchair!

She walked forward and said coolly, 'Good evening, Grandfather,' and held out her hand.

Steel grey eyes enveloped her. His handshake was brief and he gestured to the empty chair on his right, next to Ross, and waited until she was seated before saying abruptly,

'You look like your grandmother.'

'You can see it too, Father? I thought the very same thing the moment I saw her. Mother's brown eyes and the way her hair grows to a peak,' broke in Harriet eagerly.

Lucy asked, 'Who else is coming, Nunkie darling?' eyeing the empty chair beside her, and before her uncle could reply, the door opened and a voice said,

'Sorry, Philip, I hope I haven't held things up? It was an important call I couldn't possibly put off.'

Philippa froze. She knew she would have to meet him again, but on her first evening here—oh, it was too much!

Francis surveyed the occupants of the room with a swift, searching glance, betraying nothing as it passed over Philippa to rest on Lucy, who, showing animation for the first time that evening, cried,

'Oh, good, it's Francis!' and lifted her cheek for a kiss.

The two younger men exchanged greetings and Francis then crossed the room to bend to kiss Harriet, saying, 'Sorry, Harriet, I don't like mixing business with pleasure, but it happens occasionally.' He straightened and looked very definitely across at Philippa.

Philippa met his gaze steadily, a faint warmth colouring her cheeks. Mixing business with pleasure indeed! What else had Provence been? she wondered grimly. If only he didn't look so darned attractive! In evening suit with fancy white shirt and black tie he looked in full control of both himself and the situation. Lucy's delighted welcome was like turning the knife in the wound. She schooled her features to show nothing of her thoughts and lifted her chin defiantly.

Philip Ingram said, 'Francis, I understand you know my granddaughter Philippa?'

At these words Philippa's eyes widened and she glared up at Francis, who answered smoothly,

'That's right, Philip—we met in London.'

Philippa allowed a relieved sigh to escape from
parted lips. Her grandfather turned to her.

'Philippa, Francis is the grandson of an old
friend of mine, dead these many years.'

Francis touched the old man's shoulder lightly
in passing and stood before Philippa. She was
obliged to raise her eyes and found nothing but
polite, good-mannered interest in his expression.
Had he, at last, accepted that she wanted nothing
more to do with him? Her heart gave a stupid
lurch.

'It's good to see you here at Copperthwaite,
Philippa.'

'Thank you.' She waited until Francis gained his
seat and went on, 'I have such a lot to learn about
you all—tell me, please, are you also involved in
the family business, Mr Balfour?'

There was a slight pause before Francis replied
evenly, 'Yes, I am—and won't you call me
Francis? As you hear, I'm much too old a friend of
the family for us to be so formal.'

There had been nothing formal about their
lovemaking. The thought shot into Philippa's head
and was as quickly banished.

'A *sleeping* partner?' She saw the shot had gone
home by a slight tightening of his jaw and she
savoured the intoxicating delight of a small
triumph.

'Indeed not,' put in Philip Ingram, smiling.
'Francis is on the board of directors and plays an
important part in all aspects of Copperthwaite
Mills, as does Ross.' The warmth in the grey eyes
was now directed to his great-nephew. 'I'm
extremely lucky in my two youngest directors.'

And one of them, Grandfather, is extraordinarily
ambitious, thought Philippa bitterly.

CHAPTER SIX

AFTER dinner, Philip Ingram was wheeled into his suite of rooms on the ground floor, saying he would see Philippa there in half an hour.

'You mustn't let Father bully you, Philippa, my dear,' Harriet told her anxiously as they retired to the drawing-room for coffee.

'Philippa doesn't look the kind of girl to be bullied by anyone,' observed Francis, pouring out his coffee. Philippa could see he was very much at home at Copperthwaite, and a sharp stab of jealousy hit her each time Lucy made him smile. She tried to tell herself that Lucy could have him and welcome, but she knew she was fooling herself. If anything, his treachery seemed even greater now he was here, surrounded by Ingrams, and yet her heart still raced when she heard his voice, her eyes were still drawn to him whenever she was unobserved. Her own weakness fuelled the fire of her anger.

'Can't we go into Penrith or somewhere to do something?' asked Lucy plaintively, and Ross answered briskly,

'Don't look to me, sister dear. I have to be up at the crack of dawn to catch the London train—some people have to work for their living. And Philippa is about to receive the Royal Summons.' He glanced enquiringly at Francis, who turned to Lucy, asking,

'Does it have to be Penrith? Friends have just opened a pub at Bewaldeth. We could go there.'

'Lovely!' Lucy's face brightened. 'I'll go and fetch a coat,' and she ran out of the room. Philippa glanced up and found Francis watching her, a small cynical smile shaping his lips . . . as if to say, if you don't want anything to do with me there are others who are happy to oblige. With eyes locked, she demanded silently, go and enjoy yourself and see if I care! unaware of how white she had gone.

The door opened and Lucy popped her head round. 'I'm ready, Francis. 'Bye, everyone.'

Francis put down his cup and gave an indulgent laugh. 'Everything has to be instant with Lucy! Good night, Harriet. Thank you for an excellent dinner, as always. I'll see Philip before I go. Good night, Ross.' He moved towards the door, pausing by Philippa's chair. 'Are you staying on after your grandfather's birthday celebration?'

Philippa stared down at her cup. 'I don't know. It depends on my work load.'

'See as much of Cumbria as you can, it's beautiful country.'

'Why don't you come with us on Tuesday, Francis?' broke in Ross. 'We thought we'd take Philippa up Skiddaw—it's an easy mountain to climb first. Uncle has given me permission to play hookey and Lucy has fixed it with the shop.' He waited expectantly as Francis hesitated.

'Oh yes, do, Francis,' urged Lucy prettily, returning to hear the request. 'We're going to go the long way round by Dash Falls.'

'Don't you think it would be better to go from Keswick?' suggested Francis, frowning slightly, and Lucy pouted. 'Boring,' she moaned, and Philippa broke in quickly,

'The route Ross has planned suits me fine . . .

and perhaps Mr Balfour has too many commit-
ments—I wouldn't wish him to put himself out on
my behalf.'

'Tuesday will suit me perfectly,' Francis
answered smoothly, and taking Lucy's arm he
gave a general 'good night' and they left.

'Tuesday it is,' murmured Ross, picking up the
newspaper, 'that is if the weather holds. I
apologise for my sister, Philippa. She should have
stayed in on your first night here, but just lately
she can't sit still for a minute. I don't know what's
the matter with her.'

'Lucy has always been one for doing things,'
claimed Harriet placidly, picking up her knitting,
'and I'm sure Philippa doesn't want to be treated
like a guest. She's one of the family.' The needles
stopped. 'Ross—do you think Lucy and Francis
...?' She left the question hanging in the air and
looked at Ross eagerly.

Ross smiled and turned to Philippa. 'Harriet has
been trying to marry Lucy and me off for the past
five years.'

'I want to see young children running about at
Copperthwaite,' said Harriet, 'there's nothing
strange in that, is there? I'm sure Father would
like to see you both settled.' The needles began
again, but slowly, as she went on thoughtfully,
'Francis would be most suitable. I've wondered
about them before—he's always so attentive to
her.'

Lucy and Francis! The idea was unpalatable.

There was silence while Harriet brooded over
her idea, Ross read the paper and Philippa drank
her coffee, her mind made purposefully blank.
When she rose to place her cup on the table, she
asked hesitantly,

'Why is Grandfather in a wheelchair?'

Harriet sighed and dropped the knitting to her lap. 'About three years ago—it is three, isn't it, Ross? Yes, it must be—your grandfather had a fall—not a bad one, or so we thought, but it damaged the nerves in his spine. He was such a vigorous man, so fit and healthy, never a day's illness—the doctors were very concerned after the fall, but he made a remarkable recovery. He keeps surprisingly well for his age.'

'We couldn't cope without Ainsley,' said Ross, referring to the man who had come for her grandfather after dinner, Philippa realised. 'Ainsley doesn't say much,' Ross went on, 'but he's extremely able and gets on well with Uncle, which is the main thing, as his temper couldn't be said to have mellowed with the years, eh, Harriet?'

'He has much to contend with,' scolded Harriet. 'Father's perfectly reasonable if he gets his own way,' and when her two companions burst out laughing she joined in with them. 'Oh, dear—we all are, aren't we?'

'Does Grandfather still go to the Mills?' asked Philippa, and Ross snorted a laugh.

'You bet he does—not one to hand over the reins, is Uncle Philip.' This was said with fond amusement.

At that moment Ainsley came to summon Philippa to her grandfather. Outwardly composed but with her pulse racing a little, Philippa followed his dark-suited figure through the hall and down a corridor, where he stopped at the first door and tapped lightly upon it. At a command from within Ainsley opened the door and entered, saying, 'Miss Philippa, sir,' and then she was standing before her grandfather.

Philip Ingram was sitting in a winged armchair in front of the fire. He was in a dressing-gown and a plaid rug was thrown over his legs. He gestured a thin hand, and Ainsley pulled another chair forward and Philippa sat down. After bringing a silver tray with decanters and glasses to the small table within easy reach of his employer, Ainsley ascertained that there was nothing more he could do and left the room.

'Would you like a drink?' Philip Ingram began to pour one for himself. 'There seems to be a selection here. I'm having a brandy.'

'Thank you,' replied Philippa as he poised the decanter over a glass, and when the drink was passed to her she said spontaneously, 'What a beautiful glass!'

'It's Balfour—distinctive, isn't it? Francis has some good designers these days. The Balfour glass works is based in Carlisle, very near to Copperthwaite Mills.' He raised his glass. 'To a better understanding of each other.'

That was something she could drink to, and Philippa joined him. There was silence for a while as Philip Ingram stared down into his glass, the flames from the fire turning the liquid into a deep russet. 'Tell me why you've come,' he said at last, speaking carefully, as if to reassure her that the answer she gave would be accepted for consideration without bias.

Philippa said, 'I came because I was asked.'

His lips pursed a little. 'There were no other reasons?' He had a long, thin face, deeply lined, and grey hair cut close to the scalp. He must have been a tall man in his prime, thought Philippa, and he still sat upright, his grey eyes shrewd and penetrating. She sorted out her words.

'Curiosity too. As I've grown older I have felt

curious. I think, had the invitation not come, I should have sought you out eventually.'

'Always supposing I was here,' Philip Ingram observed drily. He frowned and compressed his lips. 'I didn't expect to outlive my son.' He gestured impatiently with his free hand. 'Your father and I didn't get on. We said hurtful things to each other before he left. I didn't think his going would be so final.' He shot her a look. 'At least he called you after me.'

'That was my mother's doing,' explained Philippa matter-of-factly. 'She was a gentle person who didn't like hurting people. She thought you might like the idea.'

'Hum . . . you were brought up to hate me.'

'On the contrary, whenever your name was mentioned, which I have to admit wasn't often, Dad spoke as if he'd had a happy childhood. Mother made excuses for you both.' She paused. 'I hated you without any help from my parents.'

His eyebrows met. 'You did, eh?'

'Of course. You didn't expect me to love grandparents who wanted nothing to do with me, did you? And when you didn't reply to my letter . . .' She shrugged eloquently.

His head came up. 'What letter?'

Philippa stared at him thoughtfully, then explained, 'I wrote to you after Mother died, when I was eight.' She waited a moment and went on calmly. 'You're now going to tell me that you didn't receive it, aren't you?'

'Yes, I am,' Philip Ingram replied abruptly, frowning into the fire.

She took a sip of brandy. 'Well, it's nearly twenty years ago, and there's nothing we can do about it now. Would you have replied?'

His head came round. 'Yes, I would have replied.' His eyes narrowed slightly. 'So—how long did this hatred last?'

Philippa pursed her lips pensively. 'Until my late teens, I think, and then I came to England to study and matured, I suppose. Students spend endless hours talking, you know, and my rejection was discussed along with everyone else's hang-ups.' She noticed him wince at that, and couldn't help feeling a tiny bit of satisfaction. 'I came to the conclusion that there was a case for both sides. It's quite clear that stubbornness and pride are Ingram failings. I have them myself.'

He barked a laugh. 'Got a bit of spirit, I'm glad to see! So you think I'm stubborn, do you, eh?'

'Foolish, too,' claimed Philippa calmly. 'It's never wise to issue ultimatums unless you're prepared to have them carried out.' Very clever at doling out platitudes, but you might take heed of them yourself, Philippa was telling herself sarcastically.

His eyes were, by now, mere slits. 'Stubborn, proud and foolish—that's your opinion, is it?' He grunted a laugh. 'No one can say you're buttering up to me.' He thrust forward his chin. 'Now you're here, perhaps you're wondering if I'll leave you my money?' His eyes challenged her and Philippa took her time answering.

'Surely I don't have to point out that if that's my ambition I'd have come years ago?' she said at last. '*I* know I'm not interested in your money and that's all that matters to me, but you may think what you please. I shall be quite happy to keep in touch with you, Grandfather, and I'm glad I've met my aunt and cousins, and seen the house where my father was born, but if I walked out tomorrow and never came back, my life would go on just as it has been doing. I don't need you or your money. Do you want me to go tomorrow?'

He grinned wolfishly, his face suddenly looking much younger. 'Putting all your cards on the table, aren't you? No, I don't want you to go tomorrow, dammit, and you know it. I have no intention of altering my will, but I'd like to get to know my granddaughter, even if I've only a week to do it in. This tomfool party is all Harriet's affair and I'm letting her get on with it, but I'll admit to being glad if it's made you come. Tell me about yourself,' he commanded, 'what are you doing with your life?'

'I'd better start at the beginning,' offered Philippa, laughing a little at the enormity of the question and she talked and he listened, asking a few questions now and again. When the clock struck the hour the door opened and Ainsley entered.

Philip Ingram said testily, 'Yes, what is it?'

'You asked me to come back at this time, sir.'

Philippa rose, saying, 'Goodness, is it so late? I'll come and talk tomorrow evening, if I may? Good night, Grandfather.' She crossed the hearth and stooped to kiss his forehead, catching a look of approval from Ainsley. She took with her the image of an old man, face immobile, sitting proudly in his chair, the firelight playing on the planes of his face.

Harriet met her in the hall, her hands fluttering nervously. 'How ... I mean, did Father ...?'

When the question failed to materialise, Philippa said, 'It's all right, Aunt Harriet. He tried to bully me a bit, but as Francis says, I'm not easily bullied. It was all very civilised.'

'Your father hurt him dreadfully, leaving as he did.' Harriet's voice trembled. 'I shouldn't like Father to be hurt again.'

'I promise he'll not come to any hurt through me. Do you mind if I go to bed now? I'm rather tired.'

'No, no, of course I don't mind. Off you go. Are you sure you don't want anything? A hot drink, perhaps?'

Philippa shook her head, murmured, 'Nothing, thanks,' and began to climb the stairs. At the turn she glanced back to find her aunt still there, looking up with an odd, uncertain expression on her face, rather like a small worried chipmunk, Philippa thought, and gave her a reassuring smile before she passed out of sight.

Progress with Philip Ingram was encouraging, each of them feeling their way carefully. Philippa visited his room every evening, shared a drink and talked—not specifically of the past, but of things relating to their lives and beliefs. Philippa knew her grandfather often made controversial statements to test her reaction and she had to keep her wits about her, but she spoke her mind and enjoyed the sparring. There began to grow between them a grudging respect.

Tuesday, the day planned for Skiddaw, dawned bright and Ross, scanning the sky, claimed that the day would be perfect. He turned and gave Philippa the once-over, nodding as if satisfied as he remarked, 'No matter what the weather is like when you set out you can guarantee it'll change, so it's best to be prepared.' He held out a hand. 'I'll have that waterproof in my haversack,' and his eyes again took in the chunky sweater, cord trousers and walking shoes. 'Wool socks too—

good girl!' He looked at his watch. 'I'll go and hurry up Lucy—Francis should be here in a minute.' He glanced over his shoulder and added with a grin, 'Talk of the devil!' then disappeared inside, and Philippa could hear him shouting at his sister.

A metallic grey Rover was coming over the brow of the hill and Philippa waited as it swung into the drive, her thoughts and composure held in check. Francis got out and strolled towards the house, hands in pockets, eyes lazily regarding her. He was wearing an Arran sweater that looked very much like the twin to the one Harriet was knitting at the moment, and he too was carrying a small haversack on his back.

He saw the direction of her eyes and said softly, 'Not chilled wine, French bread, pâté and goat's cheese this time—or have you wiped out all the memories?'

Philippa was saved replying by the arrival of Lucy and Ross. Lucy made a fuss of Francis and automatically took her place next to him in the Rover. Philippa joined Ross in the back. They saw few people on the drive across Uldale Fell and they parked the car just past Mirkholme and set off at an easy pace with Cockup on their right and Dash Beck over on the left. There was no need for Philippa to make sure that she and Ross walked together, Lucy commandeered Francis from the start and he made no objection.

The northern fells do not attract the crowds, Ross had told Philippa, and indeed, they did not see another soul until they had passed Dash Falls, and that was a shepherd in the distance. At midday they sat and ate sandwiches and fruit with Whit Beck babbling cold and clear within their

hearing. Before they set off again Francis came
over to Philippa and asked,

'Are you feeling fit?'

Philippa replied, 'Yes, thank you,' and when he
held out a hand to help her up from her rock seat
she pretended she had not seen it and stood up by
herself, brushing crumbs from her lap. Francis
dropped his hand and his voice remained even.
'Say, if you're not. You've done very well, even
this far. If you're feeling tired someone can go
with you into Keswick and you can wait to be
picked up.'

'I've said I'm all right,' she replied, ignoring a
slight soreness on one of her heels. She was
damned if she was going to give up!

Francis eyes her coolly for a minute, nodded,
and went back to Lucy. Ross, who had been
washing his hands in the beck, returned and they
all set off again.

The view, looking back over their shoulders at
Keswick and Derwentwater, was splendid, with
visibility clear, and had Philippa been on her own
with Ross she would have completely enjoyed the
outing. As it was, she was always aware of Lucy
and Francis, either visually ahead or verbally
behind, constantly intruding. They made it to the
top and Ross brought out a camera and took some
photographs. It was cool now, with a strong
breeze, and Philippa was glad of the windproof
anorak. Both heels were hurting by this time, but
she was on the last stretch home and thought she
could make it without complaining.

How it came about she could not tell, but after
one of their short rest spells—mainly, she
suspected, for her benefit—Philippa found herself
walking by the side of Francis, brother and sister

some yards ahead. She was not walking so easily now, but luckily Francis made no comment, merely pointing out some landmarks, making general conversation.

'Did you know that the Lake District National Park is the biggest Park in England?'

Taking her cue from him, Philippa shook her head. 'You have to have permission to build or alter, don't you?'

'Yes ... there's a special Planning Board which doles out permission and it protects footpaths and listed buildings.'

Francis had always been a good talker and before she was aware of it they had reached the road. It was decided that Ross and the two girls would walk into High Side, and Francis would go for the Rover. So—he did notice I was limping, thought Philippa, watching him go.

Back at Copperthwaite she went straight to her room and peeled off her socks and shoes. Two ugly blisters were on each heel and as she sat, wondering what to do for the best, a light tap sounded on the door and when she hobbled over and opened it, Francis walked in, carrying a bowl and cotton wool.

'I thought you could do with this,' he announced, taking over when he saw the blisters. 'Why the hell didn't you say something earlier, Philippa?' he demanded. 'I had plasters on me that would have saved the darned things from bursting. Now it'll sting like mad. Sit down.'

'I can manage perfectly well ...'

'Sit down.'

It wasn't worth arguing. She sat down and allowed him to bathe the blisters, gritting her teeth as the antiseptic stung. She looked down at the

ruffled fair hair, so easily accessible, and pushed
her hands in her pockets, out of harm's way.

Plastered and freshly socked, Philippa stood up,
saying coolly, 'Thank you, that feels much better.'

Francis' look, as he threw down the towel with
which he had been drying his hands, was shrewd
and ironic. 'Don't act the ice-maiden, Pippa,
because it won't work,' and he pulled her to him.

Off guard, Philippa had no time to protest and
her mouth was caught, soft and mobile against his,
as one hand went to the back of her head, his
fingers thrust through her hair, and the other to
the base of her spine, bringing her firmly against
him.

As she came up for air, Philippa managed,
'Francis! Let me . . .' but the outraged 'go' was
silenced.

When he finally put her away from him, Francis
gazed at the flushed cheeks and bright eyes
sparkling with anger and said with energy, 'That's
something you can remember during the long,
lonely nights!' before swinging on his heel and
leaving the room.

Philippa glared at the closed door and with a
forceful, 'Damn!' turned her back on it. Here she
came up against her reflection in the mirror and
for a moment she stared, glowering back at
herself. Was it anger that had brought the flush to
her cheeks and the light to her eyes? she demanded
silently. Keep away from him, you fool!

As the week progressed Philippa learned more
about the Copperthwaite household. Harriet was
an odd mixture of capability and fussiness. She ran
the house with the help of a small staff, the whole
geared round the welfare and happiness of her
father. As she had never married, he was the

reason for Harriet's being, and when Lucy and Ross were taken in, some of this devotion had been shared out to them. Lucy took advantage of her cousin indiscriminately, as if it was her due. Ross had more conscience, but, as he explained to Philippa, 'If it makes Harriet happy to fuss over us, then who are we to deny her?'

Ross was out of the house early each morning, driving into Carlisle to the Mills. He had, he told Philippa, worked his way up from the age of eighteen, through all the departments, and was now in control of their sales, home and abroad.

Lucy was not so easy to understand. She was friendly, but not to the extent of putting herself to any trouble on Philippa's account, but gradually Philippa realised that behind Lucy's lazy manner there was a brain and a talent and a good deal of ambition.

Copperthwaite inside belied its bleak exterior, having an old-world charm and simplicity about it. Its furnishings and brasses were lovingly cared for by Harriet and her small band of helpers, and her aunt was always ready to sit and talk about the past.

'The farm bailiff's cottage was the original house,' Harriet told Philippa during a mid-morning coffee break. 'The first wool was spun and woven there—it was only a cottage industry then, but it was the beginning of the Copperthwaite Wool Mark.' There was undisguised pride in Harriet's voice. 'As business grew our ancestors decided to build a larger house, and its basic structure hasn't been altered.'

'It's full of character,' agreed Philippa, her eyes wandering over the low ceilings, the copper warming pan and kettle and the blazing log fire.

'If you like Copperthwaite you should see Inglewood,' Lucy said carelessly, having just joined them. 'Francis Balfour's place.'

'Red sandstone, Lucy dear,' protested Harriet, 'from a different quarry altogether.'

'Yes, I know, but still old and beautiful,' insisted Lucy, and Philippa suffered the usual feeling of resentment that Lucy Fairley knew Francis better than she did herself. Silly and unreasonable, but it was there just the same.

Philippa said casually, 'I thought Francis was a Scot? Balfour is a Scottish name.'

'So it is,' agreed Harriet, 'but like many families the Balfours intermarried south of the border and settled in Cumbria.'

'Is that his home, Inglewood?' Philippa knew he had a flat in London, but he had kept Inglewood from her. Situated in Cumbria, it would have caused too many awkward questions and given his game away. Was that what Provence had been? A game?

'He's all over the place,' offered Lucy airily, 'but I guess you could call Inglewood his real home. He has business offices in Carlisle and London—a flat in London too ... which is done out in superb taste.' She gave a small, secret smile. 'I would say that, of course, as I helped him do it.'

Harriet put down her knitting and gazed fondly at her young relation, turning to Philippa to say, 'Lucy chose the colour scheme for your room—she has a way with colours.'

Philippa murmured something appropriate and disliked the sound of the London flat sight unseen.

Philip Ingram's birthday celebrations were being held in Carlisle, in the ballroom of a hotel. The Ingrams were staying there overnight and Ainsley drove them into Carlisle in the Daimler limousine, a glorious relic of the past, in which Philip Ingram was transported for his weekly visit to the Mills.

Philippa was aware of a great deal of interest in herself as she stood with the family by the side of her grandfather's chair, welcoming his guests. She felt confident enough in her appearance—she and Grace had searched London for a dress suitable for this occasion and had agreed upon a bronze silk dress in a nineteen-thirties style with a sequinned motif across one shoulder, and she had put her hair up, it seemed to fit the period.

She was introduced to friends of her father and at intervals found her eyes roaming, seeking the one person she knew had been invited whose fair head she had not yet seen.

'Looking for me?' a drawling voice asked behind her, and she swung round, saying with raised brows,

'Whatever gave you that idea?'

Francis gave a tight smile and his eyes travelled insolently over her. 'Very nice—but I don't suppose I'm the first to tell you that. I've been sent to fetch you. Your grandfather wants you to wheel him in to dinner. You'll be delighted to know I'm sitting on your other side.'

'I'm already trembling with eager anticipation,' returned Philippa shortly.

It was a grand affair. The women sparkled with colour and jewels, and the men looked smart in their evening suits, the Ingram men no exception. Harriet, whose hair was normally escaping from her bun and who had no interest in clothes, had been taken over by Lucy and Philippa. She was looking remarkably splendid in a deep burgundy velvet dress. Lucy, too, was a credit to the family, turning many heads her way as she weaved in and out of the guests, a vivid splash of emerald green.

Francis allowed the meal to reach the main course, taking advantage of the fact that Philippa was a captive audience, before asking,

'When are you going to end this farce, Pippa?'

How coolly he put the question! Philippa shot him a sparkling glare. 'I thought I asked you not to call me that?'

'I can't resist it. Anger is preferable to stony silence. But to keep the peace I'll try and remember not to call you Pippa.' He leaned back in his chair, his eyes resting upon her, and her cheeks grew warm beneath his look. 'But it's difficult, because that's how I always think of you. Memories can't be wiped out to order.'

Philippa stared down at her plate. No, memories couldn't be dismissed easily, and sitting so close, when by the turn of her head she could command instant knowledge of him, that was not easy either.

Francis gave a heavy sigh. 'I apologise for not telling you I knew Philip. I should have done. It was an error of judgment.'

'You mean you gambled and lost?' retorted Philippa. 'If I hadn't come across that newspaper article when would you have told me?'

'What happened between us has nothing whatsoever to do with your grandfather,' Francis intervened quietly.

'When?' demanded Philippa in an undertone.

Francis took a sip of his wine, considered her question, and replied, 'I would have chosen my moment carefully, I admit.'

'In bed, do you mean?' she suggested scornfully. 'Like putty in your hands?' she added, goaded by the flicker of amusement that fanned his face.

'Ah, come on now, Pippa—I can never think of you as putty!'

'It's not a joke!' Philippa ground out, the words harsh in her throat. '*You* might think so, but I don't!'

'You must agree it has its comical overtones,' he urged casually, 'and if I allowed myself to become too serious I doubt I could control my temper.' His eyes were no longer amused, but ice-blue and hard. 'I have a certain amount of patience which I'm prepared to hang on to, Philippa, but don't test it too much, will you?' Only when he was sure that she had received his message did Francis turn away and begin to talk to Harriet.

Philippa toyed with her food, her thoughts racing, and her grandfather had to say her name twice before he had her attention.

'Sorry, Grandfather, what did you say?' She collected her wits and gave him a quick smile.

'I asked if you were enjoying yourself, child, because this is for you—you know, all this. I wanted everyone to meet my granddaughter.' There was a smile in his eyes, shrewd and steady.

'You're an old fraud! You'd have had the party even if I hadn't come,' she teased. 'The place is full of owed business lunches!'

The smile moved to his lips and he waited while their plates were cleared and then asked,

'You seemed to be having a long chat with Francis. Do you like him, Philippa?'

'I hardly know him,' she answered lightly.

'I'm prejudiced, of course. Francis' grandfather was an old and close friend of mine, his father was my godson. So you see I've known him all his life. He inherited shares from his father in Copperthwaite and has shown his worth to the

Company. Then there's Ross—not quite so canny, but a worker and reliable. It's time they were both married. I married early and never regretted it, and I don't think your grandmother did either.' He took a sip of wine and wiped his mouth delicately on his napkin. 'You couldn't do better than cast your eyes over them. They're a good catch for any girl.'

'And Ross and Francis, what do they get out of it, Grandfather?' enquired Philippa mildly.

He gave a cynical smile. 'Don't denigrate yourself, child—and you're old Ingram's granddaughter . . . that's something, surely?'

'You've already pointed out that you aren't going to change your will,' offered Philippa. He was enjoying himself, she could tell by the glint in his eye. It was like playing chess with a master-player.

'So I did. Well now, an old man could change his mind, given sufficient reason, couldn't he? Think on it.'

'You're playing puppetmaster, Grandfather, and I refuse to dance to your tune,' Philippa told him severely, and changed the subject.

After the meal there was dancing to a small band. Philippa did not lack for partners—Ross claimed her more than most. She refused to count the number of times Lucy and Francis took to the floor, their fair heads close, and it did not help to see Harriet watching them too, a smile of satisfaction on her face.

Eventually word was sent to Philippa that her grandfather had gone to his room and wanted to see her. She made her way to the second floor of the hotel and Ainsley answered her knock at the door. Philip Ingram was waiting for her and she felt a swift pang, knowing she could never love him as she would wish to love him had the past been different, but she had grown to admire and respect him in many ways, and knew she should have come to Cumbria sooner.

'You wanted to see me, Grandfather?' She sat on the chair set already by his side.

Philip Ingram reached for her hand. 'Ainsley has been opening some of the presents I've received. Didn't want any, at my age I've got all I want, but nobody took any notice.' He pulled an irritated grimace, which softened as his eyes returned to her. 'But yours was special. Thank you, Philippa.'

Philippa said a little awkwardly, 'I'm glad it pleases you.'

'It's as if your grandmother is looking out of your eyes,' he remarked quietly, and glancing beyond Philippa, added, 'Can you see the likeness, Francis?'

Philippa gave a start. From out of her line of vision Francis walked forward and stood behind them, looking over their shoulders.

He said, 'Yes, Philip, I can.'

'She never reproached me, Philippa, but I knew, deep down, that it broke your grandmother's heart when your father went away.' Philip Ingram handed the photograph to Francis. 'Put it by the bed, please. No use regretting the past, doesn't get you anywhere. Off you go, child, and enjoy yourself. Francis, see her down.'

Philippa rose, bending to kiss his cheek. 'Good night, Grandfather, sleep well.'

At the door, Philip Ingram stopped them with an afterthought, calling, 'Francis—what you were asking, I give you leave, as you think best.'

Francis seemed to know what the conversation was about and nodded, without making a reply. He was silent on the way to the lift, and fortunately they were not alone as it descended, and when another guest buttonholed Francis when they reached the ballroom, Philippa made her escape.

Later, in search of fresh air, she slipped through the french windows and out on to the terrace, taking a deep breath and feeling her head clear as she did so. She leaned against the stone parapet and looked out over the moonlit gardens, wondering if her life would ever settle down to some semblance of normality. Everything seemed so complicated, and a long-drawn-out sigh escaped her lips. As she stood there, deep in thought, the music started up again inside the ballroom. It was a polka, an infectious little tune, which sent the toe of her foot tapping as she wrestled with unanswerable questions.

She gave a shiver. It was too cool to stay out long, but the freshness and the heady perfume of a late honeysuckle stayed her going.

Light spilled across the paving and the music swelled as a figure stepped from the ballroom through the same french window that she had used.

'So this is where you are. I've been looking for you.' Francis closed the window and stood barring her way.

She said pointedly, 'I was just about to go back in.'

'Running away again, Pippa?' The question was a challenging drawl.

'I'm going to find Ross—I've promised him the last waltz.'

'Ross is under the impression you've gone to bed.'

She stared at him, anger rising, colour flooding her cheeks. 'Your doing, I suppose?'

'He's soothing his hurt feelings in the arms of a pretty redhead, and enjoying himself, by the look of it.' There was grim satisfaction in his voice.

'Well, really, Francis!' exploded Philippa furiously.

'Well, really, Philippa!' mimicked Francis, and then, 'I think Ross has had too much of my *wife's* attention this evening,' and he pulled her into his arms, bringing his mouth ruthlessly down on hers.

CHAPTER SEVEN

SHE lay in his arms, a mass of confusion, the bitter-sweet, taunting word of *wife* echoing inside her head, and slowly opened her eyes to meet the triumphant searching regard of those blue eyes. Sanity returned. She thrust the palms of her hands, already spread across his chest, hard against him, crying, 'This solves nothing, Francis, nothing!' and he released her momentarily, his hands coming up to clasp her upper arms, warm through the silk of her dress. His lips twisted into a smile.

'Maybe not,' he conceded, 'but it proves plenty.'

He was, she noted, breathing heavily, and at least his damned cool had been shattered, if only briefly, which gladdened her heart.

'Do you think passion is enough?' she retorted scornfully. 'For a while, maybe, but I have to respect the man I give myself to!'

Absolute silence greeted her words. Francis lifted his hands carefully away from her and took a step back. His face was white. Philippa caught her breath on a sob. The sound of the waltz in the background was a mocking dream.

'Ah—respect!' Voice expressionless, Francis went on, 'I see. Forgive me, I've been more than a little obtuse. I'm accused of something more than knowing your grandfather.'

'You knew where to find me. It was no accident that you were at Avignon.' Philippa heard the words tumbling from her lips, challengingly, hating saying them, needing to say them.

He studied her carefully for a moment. 'Yes, I knew where to find you.'

Although she had expected it, his answer smote her cruelly. Through dry lips she asked, almost inaudibly, 'How?'

'Through Jules. I've known for some time of your friendship with Sylvie.' He saw her shiver and added abruptly, 'Let's go in, you're cold.'

'No!' Philippa backed off a pace and looked at him stonily. Francis took off his jacket and walked to her, draping it round her shoulders as he said,

'I gather I'm accused of making love to you for some specific reason. If we discount true love then it must be for gain, and if it's gain, then it must be Copperthwaite.' His voice, which had become more cynical with each observation, now became soft with conjecture. 'You believe that as you're your grandfather's heir, I'm after your inheritance.'

'I don't want to think that,' broke in Philippa angrily, 'but what other explanation is there?'

'It has, I suppose, crossed your mind that you might not be in his will?'

'Of course it has, and bad luck to you, because I'm not!'

'It might, I suppose, have crossed my mind too?'

'Francis, stop playing with me!' burst out Philippa furiously.

'My dear girl, I have no intention of playing with you.' His voice was the soft drawl, infuriating her further. 'I'm merely trying to the best of my ability to fathom the workings of your mind. You must also have realised that your grandfather hasn't long to live. To have you here under his roof at last will allow him to die in peace when the time comes. If I were a gambling man, and sometimes I am, I would lay high odds that Philip Ingram is having second thoughts. If you're not in his will I think he will reinstate you.' He smiled unpleasantly. 'It's obvious to all who see you together that he's besotted with you. It is, of course, an added bonus that you resemble his wife.'

'Don't!' whispered Philippa.

Francis gave a quick, exasperated exclamation. 'You want the truth, but don't like it when it's put to you.' He swung away and went to the window. 'I really do think you should go in. It would be a little too dramatic if I had to carry you in.' He opened the window with a flourish. Philippa made no movement. The music was coming to a finish and the curtains fluttered in the breeze.

'Have you told Grandfather about us?' she demanded, and Francis shook his head, eyeing her with watchful aloofness.

'What were you and he talking about before I came in tonight?'

There was a pause. 'Why don't you ask him?' suggested Francis smoothly.

Tightening her lips, not knowing whether to throw herself into his arms or wipe the cynical smile from his face with her hand, Philippa dragged the coat from her shoulders, flung it at him, and swept into the ballroom.

'Did you know,' said Ross, as he negotiated Carlisle's one-way system, heading for home, 'that the Scottish Border wasn't always north of the city?'

'You mean Carlisle was part of Scotland?' questioned Philippa. 'No, I have to admit that's news to me.'

'And that it boasts the only cathedral in Cumbria?'

'No, to that too—but I do know that Mary Queen of Scots fled from Scotland and took refuge in Carlisle Castle,' declared Philippa gleefully, adding, 'and if I drive through on my own I think I'd better bring a map!'

'It can be tricky,' agreed Ross, edging into an outside lane. As they waited for the lights to change he asked lightly, 'And now you've seen them, what do you think of the Copperthwaite Mills?'

'Fascinating!' declared Philippa with quick enthusiasm. 'The cloth is beautiful, and so exciting—full marks to your designers.'

'The designs are good, aren't they?' Ross spoke jauntily, and as the lights turned to green he drove on. 'We've recently acquired a new girl—Marion Parks—and she's making the buyers sit up and take notice.'

'The pretty redhead?' asked Philippa. 'I recognised her from last night—it was her at Grandfather's do, wasn't it?' She gave her cousin a quick side-glance, brows raised, and smiled inwardly as Ross nodded with admirable nonchalance. 'Is this design one of hers?' and she lifted the brown paper of the parcel on her lap and ran her fingers across the cloth inside—a mixture of browns and russets with a fine mustard line, which Philippa had chosen at Ross's insistence. 'I should hang on to Miss Parks if I were you,' she advised demurely, and Ross, giving her a quick, sharp look, replied, 'I have every intention of doing so.'

They were now out on the open road and traffic was easier, more ideal for bringing up a subject that had been on Philippa's mind for some days. She took a breath and said, 'Ross, can I ask you something, and will you answer me as honestly as you can?'

Amused, Ross answered, 'Go ahead.'

'Do you resent me coming to Cumbria?' She watched him choose his words.

'Resent? I have no right to resent you, Philippa. Lucy and I are the children of your grandfather's favourite niece, and I know he's fond of us, but we're not his grandchildren. He's done us proud all our lives and we've probably taken it rather too much for granted. In some ways your coming has made us both sit up and take stock. I'm glad for the old man's sake that you've come. He doesn't say much, but I can tell it means a lot to him, you being here.' He paused, frowning slightly. 'So no, resentment isn't what I'm feeling, but I wouldn't be human if I didn't admit to speculation as to what's going to happen now.'

'Nothing's going to happen,' Philippa told him crossly. 'I shall go back to London in a couple of days' time and get on with my life. I'll come back to Copperthwaite if I'm asked.'

'Some things happen without our knowledge or our control,' said Ross drily, and Philippa said quickly and earnestly,

'You're thinking about the business and, I suppose, the house, and I don't blame you. Do you honestly think Grandfather would cast you off just because I've arrived on the scene? For heaven's sake, Ross! What do *I* know about the wool trade?'

Ross shrugged. 'One part of me thinks, no, he wouldn't, the other part takes one look at you, the image of your grandmother, and I'm not so sure.

Uncle has a guilt complex about your father which he could ease through you.'

'Not to the extent of hurting you and Lucy, Ross. I've been talking to him and I've made it quite plain that I'm not interested in anything but getting to know you all. I've told him I won't live at Copperthwaite, that I have my own life and intend to go on just the way I always have. Grandfather has too much of a sense of duty to do anything silly, and he's too passionately involved with the mills to put them in jeopardy.' She paused. 'And in any event, you and Francis have some power in the Company, haven't you?'

'We would both follow the Old 'Un's wishes.'

Philippa allowed him to take a tricky corner and then said mildly, 'I'll tell you this, Ross—I have no intention of marrying you.'

Ross turned a startled face her way and burst into laughter. 'Oh, lord, has the Old 'Un been on to you too?'

'He has. You can't blame him, it would solve everything, wouldn't it? I could grow very fond of you, Ross, as a cousin . . .'

Ross grinned. 'But not as a husband, eh? There's someone else, isn't there?'

'Yes, but it's complicated. And you?'

Ross pursed his lips. 'Yes, but it's early days yet.' He flicked her a teasing glance. 'Not that I couldn't take you on—given encouragement.' His voice went evilly dramatic. 'Especially if I knew you were going to inherit Copperthwaite, my dear!'

'Thank you very much,' responded Philippa, laughing indignantly. She paused and went on hesitantly, 'Could you do that, Ross? Marry for money?'

Ross checked to see she was serious, and shrugged. 'We all marry for gain in some form or another. Perhaps you're not aware of it at the time ... companionship, security, possessiveness, even gratitude. Pecuniary gain is always looked down on, but if it's purely incidental and real feelings are involved, then it doesn't matter, does it?'

Philippa lapsed into silence which Ross did not interrupt. Incidental! But Francis had admitted to her that it was no accident that they had met, that he had planned it! He need not have admitted it. He could have lied to her and she would not have found out, for Jules would never have betrayed his cousin. So why had Francis admitted it? Her head was beginning to ache and she couldn't think straight any more. She was glad when Ross began to make small talk, and she was obliged to answer. It stopped all the whys and wherefores buzzing around in her head.

Ross said, 'The birthday went off well last night, I thought. Perhaps Harriet can relax now. She's been a mass of nerves this past week. I think your coming steamed her up too.'

'She's very fond of you and Lucy,' observed Philippa, and he nodded. They were approaching Caldbeck and he slowed for a pedestrian crossing. Schoolchildren were waiting and Ross signalled them to cross. How much easier, thought Philippa, if I'd fallen in love with Ross. How nice and tidy.

'We're the children Harriet never had,' Ross went on, as he gathered speed.

'Has she never had the chance to marry?' asked Philippa curiously.

'Not to my knowledge. It seems she was never the same after the other brother died. You knew about that?'

'Yes, but no details.'

'I know only that he was drowned in a tarn out on Caldbeck Fell. There's hundreds of pools not big enough to be on a map but big enough for a nine-year-old to drown in. Harriet took his death badly ... his name was Philip, after your grandfather ... and she was ill for a time. It's not talked about.' He peered through the windscreen towards the house which had just come into view. 'That looks like Francis' Spider!' He frowned. 'And Dr Bell's Ford. I wonder what's up?'

Francis met them in the hall to say that Philip Ingram had been taken ill. 'He wasn't feeling well when we left Carlisle this morning, but insisted on coming home. I followed Ainsley in case it was needed to chase off for a doctor en route.'

'What's the matter with him?' asked Philippa, beating Ross to the question by a few seconds.

Francis lifted his hands and dropped them again, his face troubled. 'Exhaustion? Excitement? He's kept going for so long and now his body is forcing him to realise his limitations.' He ran fingers through his hair and rubbed the back of his neck. 'He's as clear as ever in his mind.' He shook his head wonderingly, grimacing a smile. 'When I suggested we took him to hospital, he insisted he was going to die in his own bed.'

Philippa suddenly realised how close Francis was to her grandfather. He really loved the old man!

'Is Doc with him now?' asked Ross, striding to the door, and Francis called after him, 'I think he's with Harriet. She needed attention.'

With Ross's going, silence fell between them. Francis walked to the window and stared out.

After a moment, Philippa asked quietly, 'Will he die?' and he replied without turning,

'No, but he hasn't long.' He glanced over his shoulder. 'A few weeks, perhaps.'

Philippa sank into a chair and leaned her head back, closing her eyes. She said heavily, 'I'm sorry. You're fond of him.'

'Yes, I am.' The reply was almost curt.

How her head ached! It was her own fault. All she had to do was to get up and walk over to him and go into his arms. She would lay her head on his chest and he would fold his arms round her . . . and they would find again the magic they had lost. She wanted to share his grief, wanted to be included in everything he felt and did. Wanted to catch his eye in a crowd and pass those secret messages known only to lovers. She wanted to share his bed and comfort him when he needed comforting, and laugh with him and talk with him and bear his child . . .

She ached to go over and could not. After what had been said last night, she could not go to him. There was something in his face that daunted her, and with a heavy heart she realised that she might even have left it too late.

'You go tomorrow.' His voice was expressionless as he turned from the window, and opening her eyes she found indifference on his face.

'Yes, unless Grandfather worsens. I have some important jobs coming up which I shall cancel if I have to.'

Any more conversation between them was stopped by Ross entering the room, saying, 'Doc's just left. He's sedated Harriet and confined her to bed. Uncle's satisfactory, but Doc says we must remember he's an old man whose body is winding down.' He pushed his hands in his pockets, scowling down at the carpet. 'Bit of a shock, isn't it? He's never seemed old before, and now he does. He looks frighteningly frail. Are you staying, Francis? Cook wants to know.'

Francis shook his head. 'I must go, Ross. Will you keep me posted? I'll be at my London number until Thursday and then I fly to the States.' He paused in his walk to the door, adding, 'If Philip ... if you need me, the office will be able to contact me.' The two men exchanged looks of shared grief and then Francis turned to Philippa, saying briefly, 'Goodbye—have a safe journey home,' and then he was gone.

Ainsley came to fetch Philippa, as usual, after dinner. She asked anxiously as they walked to her grandfather's room,

'Is he well enough to see me tonight, Ainsley?'

'Mr Ingram wishes to see you now, Miss Philippa. If you stay for a bit it can't do him any harm, and not seeing you might give him a restless night.' Ainsley smiled encouragingly as he ushered her into the bedroom.

Philip Ingram was propped up on pillows, and as she approached he opened his eyes and she sat on the chair next to the bed and took his hand in hers, saying gently,

'Hey, what's this? Trying to get attention?'

He gave a dry smile. 'I doubt I'll see the New Year in, child, but I'm ready. The spirit's willing but the flesh is weak.' He glared at her. 'So no damned-fool pussyfooting pretending, eh?'

'No pussyfooting, Grandfather,' consented Philippa softly.

'You're off to London tomorrow, I suppose? Don't know what you see in the place—ugh! Can't stand it. Too big, too crowded. Nobody knows anybody.' He stopped, taking a rest, and went on, 'Now up here you can breathe. Everyone knows their own business and yours too!' He gave a breathy laugh. 'Or thinks they do.' He looked at her keenly. 'Are you glad you came?'

'Yes, Grandfather.' Philippa hesitated. 'I want to say something, but I don't quite know how to go about it.'

'Straight out, that's the best way.'

Philippa looked him full in the face, her voice serious. 'I don't want to cause trouble—for Lucy and Ross.' She stared at him, willing him to understand. His face cleared and he closed his eyes.

'I shall do what I have to do.' He patted her hand. 'Don't worry, child.' He was silent for a while and Philippa wondered if he'd fallen asleep, and then he said, 'Harriet's the problem—always has been. But I can't worry about her now. Francis has promised to do his best.'

Philippa said suddenly, 'Grandfather, you remember when I came to say good night to you at the hotel and Francis was with you?'

'I remember.'

'You'd been talking together and before we left you granted Francis a request he had made to you before I'd arrived.'

'Well?' His eyes opened and he stared unblinkingly at her. 'Curious, are you?'

'Francis said I could ask you what you meant,' she explained lamely, the colour rising to her cheeks beneath his shrewd eyes.

'Huh! You'll have to ask him again.' Philip Ingram waved a dismissive hand. 'I'd made him promise something and released him from it, that's all. Damn fool things, promises. Especially deathbed ones.' His eyes glared. 'I shan't demand any. The most ordinary promises become extraordinary the minute they're given—remember that.' He lapsed into silence, once more saying firmly, 'There's two kinds of people, Philippa. The ones that keep 'em, and the ones that don't.'

'And Francis keeps them,' stated Philippa slowly. She sat for a moment, thinking. 'Perhaps he ought to give me a few lessons,' she murmured at last, remembering the promises she had made in the Town Hall at Avignon in front of the Mayor, with Sylvie and Jules as witnesses. Remembering the bright sunshine as they came out of the building into the Place de l'Horloge, and the celebratory meal they had with Sylvie and Fabien, and the newly engaged Lisette and Jules.

She lifted her grandfather's hand to her cheek and said softly, 'I want to tell you something, Grandfather, about Francis and me. Something you'll be pleased to learn.'

She spoke quickly, unburdening herself, and when she had finished her grandfather made no judgment, merely held her hand a little tighter, saying soothingly, 'Ask him to explain again, Philippa.'

Philippa went to bed, strangely happy for the first time in weeks.

'As I thought,' said Grace, twenty-four hours later when Philippa had brought her up to date. 'Just a foolish, stubborn old man.'

'Dad was just the same,' pointed out Philippa reasonably. 'They were too much alike—each wanting his own way.' She gave a small, exasperated sigh. 'If Dad hadn't had the bad luck to fall off that cliff he could have come to

Copperthwaite with me. I know I could have talked him round.'

'No good stubbing your toe against fate, my girl. All you'll end up with is a sore foot.'

Philippa smiled reluctantly and made herself more comfortable in the armchair. It had poured with rain all the way down the motorway and she was glad to be home.

'I can't say you look as though your week away has done you much good,' observed Grace, looking at her niece critically and noting the dark shadows beneath her eyes.

'I admit to not sleeping too well, but I had things on my mind.'

'I wonder if your husband would be gratified to learn that he's termed a "thing"?' Grace asked slyly, and Philippa pulled a face.

'Since telling Grandfather I feel much better,' admitted Philippa. She hesitated and went on slowly, 'Now all I have to do is ask Francis about this promise he made—if he'll let me.'

'Oh, he'll let you,' claimed Grace comfortingly, 'but he'll choose his own time and place, if I know anything.'

'I'm not so sure. You didn't see his face when I virtually accused him of marrying me for Copperthwaite,' responded Philippa, and sank into a depressed silence.

One day to catch up on correspondence—there was a long letter from Sylvie begging for news—and to sort out the telephone messages on the answering machine, and then Philippa started out the following day for the business premises of Dronfield & Farnsworth Incorporated, importers of wine from France, Italy and Spain. She had done work for them before, but had never sat in on a meeting, which was what she was to do that day.

Peter Farnsworth, with whom she had had previous contact, greeted her warmly, allowing an admiring glance to pass over her tweed Prince of Wales check suit and its accompanying red shirt. As she took off the matching red felt hat and ran fingers through her hair, he said,

'I wish more women wore hats. I love 'em.' He paused and his smile deepened. 'Hats, I mean. Better not admit to loving women or my wife will be after me!' He glanced at his watch and indicated for Philippa to walk with him. 'The boardroom is a gloomy place at the best of times and October seems to be foretelling a harsh winter, don't you think? Bitterly cold wind today.' Not really expecting an answer, he led the way and ushered Philippa into a room in which a highly polished oval table with chairs set round in perfect symmetry dominated. Past Presidents gazed sombrely down from the walls. A middle-aged woman was sitting at a side table and was introduced as the minutes secretary, and Philippa took her place, noting the glass of water within easy reach, together with blotter, paper and pen. This format was duplicated all round the table.

Peter Farnsworth excused himself and returned some seconds later with the rest of the meeting in tow. Philippa was introduced to them all, taking special note of two Frenchmen, the purpose of her being there, father and son, the Messieurs Bouviers, who were delighted to be able to talk in their own language.

'Ah, good, here he is now. We can begin.' Peter Farnsworth's exclamation filtered through. The empty chair at the table was now apparent as members had taken their places, and all heads turned to the latecomer. It was Francis who now walked into the room.

Philippa sat riveted to her chair, the breath knocked out of her, and realising that her mouth had dropped open she shut it quickly. She hardly knew what she was feeling as she watched him shake hands, finishing with the Bouviers, speaking to them in his fluent French. At last he turned to Philippa.

'Good morning,' Francis said calmly. 'If there's anything you don't understand, ask, won't you?'

'Thank you, I will.' The words came out somehow, and she felt her cheeks grow warm under his impersonal gaze. How could he stand there and look at her as if she were a stranger? Her heart gave a lurch and pain shot through her. She lowered her eyes, thankful when he moved away and took his seat.

The meeting began and for a few minutes Philippa found she was flustered by Francis' presence, but gradually she settled down, hoping her nervousness had not been apparent. She was acutely aware of him, all the time, sitting quietly— he had the capacity for stillness—thoughtfully considering the business put before them.

When a break for coffee came, Philippa was given the chance to feast her eyes on him as he stood talking on the other side of the room to the Bouviers. Grey suit, pink shirt, grey striped tie—he looked modern, immaculate and absolutely wonderful. He was sporting his listening expression, and Philippa suddenly realised that Francis was a good listener. He had let her talk during their time together in Provence. He must have known a little of what she had to tell, but he had been genuinely interested, she knew that now, and it had been therapeutic for her to spill it all out.

She lifted her eyes from the coffee cup again, allowing them to find him. He had a half-smile on his lips and his arms were folded across his chest, body relaxed. His gaze drifted away from the Frenchmen and met hers, fully, for the first time. Everything and everyone paled into insignificance and all Philippa could hear was the thumping of her heart in her ears. One brow rose as he studied her thoughtfully and her cheeks grew warm, but she held his look.

The secretary's voice intruded with, 'Another cup of coffee, Miss Ingram?'

Philippa refused with a quick smile and wondered what would happen if she said, Actually, my name is Balfour, Mrs Francis Balfour ... That would shake his infuriating cool—or would it? With Francis you never could tell.

The meeting resumed. Philippa had always known Francis was clever, that he had an agile brain and a fluent command of facts and figures, but it was something else, seeing him in action. He controlled the meeting, allowing a point to be argued until it had reached saturation and then arbitrated, summing up until agreement was met. At the close, Philippa was commandeered by Monsieur Bouvier junior, who was trying to persuade her to join him for lunch, and when she looked round the room she realised that Francis was no longer present. Disappointment swept over her beyond all expectation. She could hardly be civil to poor Monsieur Bouvier and choked off his advances with unladylike shortness, excused herself and went in search of Peter Farnsworth.

'Has Francis . . . Mr Balfour gone?' she asked, already knowing the answer but deep down hoping against hope she would be proved wrong.

'Yes, I'm afraid he had to dash . . . he's due at Heathrow in an hour for his flight to America.' Peter Farnsworth looked at her with some curiosity. 'Francis asked me to look after you, take you to lunch. He apologises for not taking you himself, but that's my good fortune.' He waited a moment, nonplussed by her lack of response, and added carefully, 'You do know each other, don't you?'

Philippa pulled herself together and said hurriedly, 'Yes, yes, we do,' and fought down the impulse to shout: I'm his wife, you idiot! realising, with shock, that that was the second time within an hour that she had had to resist the temptation.

His face cleared and he smiled. 'I thought I was right. That's why I didn't introduce you both. After all, it was Francis who put us on to you in the first place.'

Philippa stared, eyes widening. '*Francis* did?' Her voice rose incredulously.

He clapped a palm against his forehead. 'Whoops! Didn't you know? Perhaps I've let the cat out of the bag!'

'But I've been doing work for you for three years,' protested Philippa, and he nodded, totally unaware that he had said anything fantastic.

'And very pleased we are with your work too. Now, how about lunch?'

'I'm sorry, but,' and Philippa looked vaguely round for her things, 'I'm already engaged, a business lunch with a publisher which I can't put off.' But I would have, for Francis, she was thinking. Three years? I can't believe it—Peter Farnsworth's got it wrong, he must have!

She asked abruptly, 'Are you sure? About Francis recommending me to you?'

Peter Farnsworth looked at her thoughtfully. 'Yes, Philippa, I'm sure. You see? *Philippa!* I always think of you as Philippa, not Miss Ingram, because that's what Francis has always called you. So you see . . .' His voice trailed and his eyes began to twinkle, taking in her rising colour. 'Never underestimate him, Philippa. He's a clever, devious devil at times.'

'Three years ago, Grace!' Philippa stood in the middle of her aunt's study, her face flushed, her hair wild where she had ran impatient fingers through it, bewilderment rising in her voice. 'How did he know what I was doing three years ago? Know me well enough to recommend me to Peter Farnsworth? We only met in May, for heaven's sake! Why didn't he tell me?'

'Why don't you ask him?' mimicked Grace drily.

Philippa ground her teeth. 'I would, only he's over the Atlantic right this minute. Oh!' and the exclamation exploded as a long-drawn-out groan of frustration.

'He's left a message,' Grace said casually, and Philippa spun round.

'Who?' She eyed her aunt with suspicion.

'Your Francis. In the kitchen. I think he's determined to play havoc with my allergies.'

'Not more poppies?' exclaimed Philippa incredulously. 'At this time of the year?'

'No, not more poppies. Why don't you go and have a look?' Grace sounded amused, and giving her an exasperated look Philippa swept in to the kitchen and Grace heard her cry,

'Oh, my goodness!' and then, laughter breaking through, 'Oh, my goodness!'

'Exactly,' said Grace, joining her. 'I hope your husband doesn't think I'll look after the thing while you're traipsing all over the world at his heels.'

'Oh, you beauty, you little beauty!' and Philippa sank to her knees, her eyes shining.

'Little? Well, he might be—yes, I've ascertained he's a he—he might be little at the moment, but they grow! Boy, do they grow!'

Philippa took the Afghan hound's head between her hands and they stared at each other solemnly, the pup's tail wagging tentatively at the tip.

'The man who delivered him said he had orders to come tomorrow to see if we're going to keep him. I gather we are. Correction—you are. Dogs make me sneeze, you know that.'

'You're beautiful,' crooned Philippa, turning a shining face upwards to demand, 'Grace, isn't he beautiful?'

'Yes, yes, we agree he's beautiful. He's also beautifully mannered for a pup. He watered the old rug and not the new one. Wasn't that clever of him?'

Philippa began to giggle. 'I wonder what his name is?'

'Wonder no more.' Grace rummaged in a box. 'His pedigree is here somewhere—ah, yes, let me see . . .' She beamed a smile and began to laugh. 'His name is Beau François of Inglewood, out of Paladin of Greystoke and Beautiful Star. Beau François! You can hardly call him Francis, can you? Very confusing, so it's got to be Beau, which suits him perfectly. The man left a list of instructions and a box of foodstuff. Highly organised, this Francis of yours.'

CHAPTER EIGHT

GRACE, grumbling goodnaturedly, agreed to have Beau while Philippa was in Italy.

The trip went as planned, without incident, and on the return journey as the aircraft circled the airport prior to landing, Philippa was already thinking ahead, planning how to contact Francis. Whenever she thought of him, which was often, she was filled with a mixture of excitement and apprehension.

Grace was waiting as she came out of Customs, and one look at her aunt's face caused Philippa to ask urgently,

'Grace, what's wrong? Francis . . .?'

'No, my dear, it's your grandfather.'

A feeling of relief, followed quickly by one of regret, swept over Philippa.

'He died two days ago,' Grace went on. 'There was no time to send for you, and Ross and I decided there was no point in bringing you home. The funeral is tomorrow.'

'I must go,' said Philippa.

Grace answered, 'Of course you must go, but by train, my dear, not by car. The weather forecast isn't good—they've had snow and blizzards in the north, and the prospect for the next few days is the same. Ross will meet you off the train if you'll let him know which one. There's one from Euston to Carlisle which gets in around eight. You can have a meal at home and then I'll run you to the station.'

Philippa left all the arrangements to Grace and found herself sitting in the railway carriage going north almost before she had time to catch her breath. She felt sad at the news of her grandfather's death. It seemed unfair, just when she was getting to know him. She wondered how Harriet was taking it. Badly, no doubt.

The thought suddenly struck her that Francis would be there, and she felt a lifting of tension and settled back and pondered what she would say to him when she saw him.

At Carlisle station she peered along the platform for a sign of Ross. She could not see him, and as she handed in her ticket she came to the conclusion that the weather must have worsened and he had been held up. She would telephone Copperthwaite and find out what was happening.

As she began to make her way towards the telephone kiosk a figure suddenly barred her way and she stopped in her tracks. He was wearing a tweed overcoat, collar upturned, snowflakes glistening on the shoulders, and the crown and brim of a felt hat which was pulled down over one brow.

'Francis!' His name escaped her lips on a breath, the blood rushed to her face and then left it just as quickly. He seemed to have grown taller and thinner, and he was pale—his usually enigmatic face hollowed and shadowed. She swayed slightly and his hands came out of the pockets of the coat and grabbed her by the arms. They stared into each other's eyes and then she was in his arms, crushed until the breath nearly left her and his mouth came down, fiercely, hungrily, and she was returning the kiss with all the pent-up longing and remorse spilling out.

As they broke away, Francis said, 'No more

play-acting, Pippa. I can't take any more.'

Philippa lifted her hands to his face, replying almost incoherently, 'Nor can I. Oh, Francis, hold me!' and she was gathered into his arms again, her face buried in the rough material of his coat. She gave a long-drawn-out sigh and murmured, 'Oh, you don't know how I've longed for this!'

'So have I, but not quite under these conditions, when there's very little I can do about it.' The wry amusement in his voice brought her head up and she began to laugh, aware suddenly of the hustle and bustle of the station around them and the occasional protracted glances of passers-by. She felt drunk with happiness and amazingly carefree.

'What do you suggest?' she asked him, her lips curving into a mischievous smile.

'That you come home, where you belong,' Francis replied challengingly, picking up her case and swinging her towards the exit, a proprietorial arm around her.

The Rover was parked awaiting, snow thick across the windscreen, and while Philippa settled herself Francis cleared all the windows and then took his seat, the thick coat hampering his movements. When the door was secure he turned to her and said grimly, 'I love you, Pippa, and whatever's in that damn will tomorrow matters not one jot—do you understand?' and he cupped a hand round her neck and pulled her to him, kissing her almost angrily. When their lips parted he searched her face, eyes intense, his breathing impaired. He released her abruptly and gripped the wheel, the knuckles showing white, grinding out between clenched teeth, 'I promised myself I'd be gentle, but you make it so bloody difficult!'

'I don't want you to be gentle.'

His head came round at that and brown and
blue eyes locked. Without speaking, Francis
started the engine. The wipers cleared the driving
snow and as they gained the main road, Philippa
asked,

'What happened to Ross?'

'Nothing happened to him.' Francis gave a
tight smile. 'I didn't knock him down to take his
place, if that's what you mean, although I would
have done had it proved necessary. I reckon Ross
guessed as much. Anyway, I told him that I'd pick
you up and would he let me know what train you
were arriving on. I also told him not to expect you at
Copperthwaite until tomorrow afternoon.'

'What did he say to that?'

'Nothing.' Francis flicked her an unrepentant
glance. 'I was not prepared to argue, and my manner
gave some indication as to how serious I was.'

'You mean you were your normal arrogant,
bossy self?' Philippa murmured, and he gave a
short laugh.

'Possibly. Ross isn't stupid. He accepted the
implications and we left it at that, without discussion. I shall apologise for my high-handed-
ness when I'm in a calmer frame of mind.'

Exultation swept over Philippa. That infuriating
self-control was shattered—he did love her! The
cool, urbane Francis Balfour was gone and she
was seeing raw, truthful emotion, nothing hidden
or camouflaged. She hugged the knowledge to her,
as incredulous joy spread through her.

'Where are you abducting me to, Francis?' she
murmured.

'Home—Inglewood. It's been waiting for you
long enough—and so have I.' He shot her another
challenging look. 'I would have come for you in

any event. My patience had come to an end even before I got your message.'

'What message was that?' she asked cautiously.

'Don't come the innocent, Pippa. I came back from the States and Philip sent for me. You'd told him all about us. I knew you'd never have told him if there was no chance for us—not even to make him happy. I made myself wait until I reached home and then rang you, only to find you were in Italy, and I had some more waiting to do.'

'You're quite good at it,' observed Philippa mildly, and Francis said with swift grimness,

'Not any more.' He peered ahead through the driving snow. 'Not far now. Nearly home.'

Home. Philippa wriggled with happiness. She sneaked a look at him. Every line and curve of his face she knew intimately, carried with her all these weeks of denial. It gave her exquisite pleasure to indulge herself now. Francis felt her eyes upon him and turned to her, and they exchanged looks, and he muttered,

'Damn this snow—just when I want to get you home!'

Outside, Philippa became aware that open country had changed to forest land, and then Francis turned into a gateway and a house loomed up out of the darkness in the beam of the headlamps. A light was burning in the porch, and Francis murmured with satisfaction,

'Good—Mrs Tulley has been in, bless her.' He pulled to a halt, explaining, 'The Tulleys farm down the road and keep an eye on the place while I'm away. Stay still until I get the front door open.'

Philippa watched him carry her case indoors, the headlamps left on to illuminate the path. Light from the hall spilled out and then Francis returned, ploughing his way back through the snow, opening the car door and helping her out. She was wearing low-heeled boots, but even so was glad of his support, for the snow was deep. The cold was intense, yet she was hardly aware of it. She seemed to be glowing from inside and the feel of his arm around her, steadying her, delighted her. At the porch Francis stopped and she looked at him questioningly, a gasp escaping her lips as she was swung up into his arms.

'Francis! What on earth . . .?'

'I'm carrying you over the threshold.' The snow was settling on them, like confetti.

'You idiot!' Philippa folded her arms round his neck and kissed him. 'You romantic idiot,' she repeated softly, resting her cheek against his.

'That's not the general image I like to put about,' Francis answered drily, carrying her through into the house and kicking the door shut with a foot, 'and I'd be grateful if you'd keep it to yourself.' He let her feet fall gently to the floor, retaining his hold of her. 'There's enough food in the house to feed an army and enough booze in the cellar to float a battleship, so don't worry about being marooned by the blizzard.'

'Who says I'm worried?' quipped Philippa.

'There should be a good fire going, through there. Go in and get warm while I put the car away.' Francis stood for a moment, looking at her before backing slowly away and then out through the front door. Philippa smiled and wandered into the room he had indicated. There was a good fire, but she did not need one. The blood was coursing through her veins and she put up a hand to her face, feeling the heat in her cheeks. Giving a choking laugh, she took off her coat and put it across the back of a chair, then looked around her with interest. It was a large room, beautifully furnished with what looked like genuine antique furniture, one wall completely covered in bookshelves. Wall-lights gave an intimate atmosphere, helped by floor-length curtains at each end in apricot velvet. Two huge sofas faced each other, either side of the stone fireplace, in a neutral material, and an Indian rug separated the two. Some pictures on the walls, to be inspected later at leisure, and some interesting sculptured pottery figures were all she had time to see before Francis returned, minus his outdoor things. He crossed to the fire, holding his hands forward for warmth. He was wearing a thick navy-blue sweater which hung round hips clad in matching cords. As he straightened Francis turned to look at her, and a strange awkwardness fell between them.

'Would you like a drink? Something to eat?' Francis lifted a hand in the direction of a corner cupboard.

A light sprang to Philippa's eyes and she wanted to shout out with happiness. Was this *Francis* who was incredibly unsure of himself?

'For someone who's too clever by half,' she said in a shaking voice, 'you're awfully dumb where my appetite's concerned, just at this particular moment.' She did not need to say any more. He was across the space between them and she was in his arms, and they were saying words that had been held in for too long, words that tumbled out, incoherent, breathless, until they fell silent at the same time, drawing away slightly to gaze into each other's eyes. The exultant laughter came then, delighting in each other.

Slowly, savouring every second, Francis went to

the light switch and the room was illuminated by
the bright orange flames of the fire. They
undressed each other, fingers dealing delicately
with zips and buttons and their reunion was fierce,
born of a separation which had, perhaps, been
necessary to allow a coming to terms with their
dependence upon each other.

The growth of feeling and blossoming love had,
in Provence, been touched with a magic that by its
very swiftness made them vulnerable.

'What a fool I've been,' murmured Philippa
contentedly.

Francis gave a rueful laugh and caught her hand
and brought it to his lips. 'I don't come out with
much credit, Pippa love. Philip reckoned you must
have bewitched me, and he wasn't far wrong.' He
became serious, gazing intently into her eyes. 'I
didn't intend to sweep you off your feet like I did,
it just happened, and I didn't want to spoil
anything with explanations. Stupid, I know, but I
wanted you on my own terms, without any
complications due to your family. So far as I was
concerned, it was just you and me.'

'I think you could say it was that,' teased
Philippa, smoothing her fingers across his shoulder,
needing to touch him, feel him close, to make sure
this was all real.

'You were mine, and I was damned if I was
going to wait while I persuaded you that the
Ingrams weren't the baddies you'd believed them
to be all your life.'

'You've got an awful lot of explaining to do,'
accused Philippa, 'and I'm hungry.' She felt him
shake with laughter.

Francis raised himself on one elbow and looked
down at her humorously. 'Here, wrap yourself in

this while I go and get you a dressing-gown,' and he drew a tartan blanket from a chair and draped it round her. Struggling into a sweater that seemed to have everything inside-out, he grinned at her. 'As for being hungry, you have your priorities in perfect order. We shall have a bottle of claret—a Château Haut-Brion—which I've been saving for just such an occasion as this. It is, perhaps, a little grand for Mrs Tulley's excellent "tattie pot", a Cumbrian delicacy which I hope hasn't spoiled for the waiting. And then we shall talk.'

This promise was given halfway out of the room. A few minutes later he returned, carrying a striped black-and-tan towelling dressing-gown. He held out his hands and pulled Philippa to her feet. He helped her into it, and watching her tie the belt, said roughly, 'I suppose I shall get used to seeing you here. I've dreamed of it long enough.'

Philippa murmured, 'Oh, I'm real enough,' and wound her arms round his waist, snuggling close. A thought struck her. 'Francis, I haven't thanked you for Beau! He's a darling.'

Francis laughed. 'I thought he was rather appropriate as a reminder of me. Now! Time you started learning where everything is. I'll fetch the wine, you find glasses in that cabinet over there.'

They ate informally by the fire and then Philippa curled up on the sofa in the shelter of Francis' arms. She slipped a hand inside his sweater, spreading her palm over his heartbeat. The thud, thud was a most reassuring phenomenon, giving credence to the fact that he too was for real. She said thoughtfully, 'Francis?'

'Mmm?' Francis moved a few inches into a more comfortable position so that he could see her face easily.

'Why did you come to Provence? Did Grandfather ask you to?'

He shook his head. 'No, that was all my idea. I knew you'd been sent an invitation and suspected that Philip desperately wanted you to come, so I thought I'd do a spot of checking up. I certainly didn't realise what I was getting myself into.' He smiled into her upturned face. 'I need to go back a bit for you to understand wholly.' He frowned slightly, assembling his thoughts. 'I saw your grandfather the morning before he died. He sent for me. Harkness, the solicitor, was there . . .'

'Oh, Francis, I do hope he wasn't changing his will!' Philippa sat up in alarm and Francis gently pulled her back to him.

'My dear girl, your grandfather was entitled to do whatever he wished. And he wasn't changing it, he was merely adding a codicil. He knew he hadn't long to live. He made me go over again how we had met—he was enormously happy about us, Pippa—his granddaughter and the grandson of his closest friend.'

'I wish I could have had a bit longer knowing him,' Philippa murmured sadly.

'He felt the same, and told me it was difficult to look back and see any sense in what had happened between himself and your father. It was, of course, very different thirty years ago. The north of England is a harsh country and demands hard living, and painting in those days was not considered to be work, and certainly not a means to earn a living. I think Philip thought your father would soon find that out and return. He was angry and disappointed when Robert didn't, but he didn't cut Robert off completely. He traced you all eventually to France and kept a watching brief.'

'You mean Grandfather knew what was happening to us all the time?' The words came out slowly as Philippa took in the implications.

Francis lifted a hand and smoothed back the hair from her face, saying gently, 'There's more to come.'

Philippa looked into Francis' face as if searching for reassurance. 'I can hardly believe it,' she breathed. 'Did Dad know?'

'Not to my knowledge.'

A thought struck her and she demanded, 'Why didn't Grandfather answer my letter, then?'

'Ah, yes, your letter. Philip did ask me, if it were possible, that we keep this bit to ourselves. It seems that your letter did reach Copperthwaite, but not your grandfather.'

'Someone took it.' Philippa considered this and then said pensively, 'Aunt Harriet?'

'Yes, I'm afraid so,' confirmed Francis, frowning slightly. 'It made painful telling for Philip, but he wanted you to know that he hadn't refused your cry for help, which is what that letter was really all about, wasn't it?'

'Yes, I suppose it was, although I didn't ask for anything.' Philippa pulled a rueful face. 'If you only knew how I waited and waited for a reply!' She laid her head on his shoulder and urged, 'Go on.'

'I need to fill you in with some family history. You remember that your grandparents had a son, called Philip, who died? You can imagine what his arrival meant—the Ingram name and tradition could be carried on. Harriet was born two years later and became young Philip's adoring slave. As he grew up Philip showed an amazing interest in the mills, begging to be taken at every opportunity.

He was a bright boy, a bit of a dare-devil, and spoilt by everyone. Now we come to the tragedy which must have changed all their lives, your father's too. He was only a baby at the time, but the result affected him later. Philip and Harriet were not allowed out on the fells alone and they were forbidden to swim in the tarns even when accompanied—some are extremely deep and even when the sun is shining the water is cold. Philip was nine and Harriet seven and they set off by themselves for a picnic. They knew the fells well, of course, and often went out with the shepherds as your grandfather encouraged them to know the land and what went on in it. However, this time they went out without permission. It was hot and when they came to the tarn Philip said he was going to swim. He was a strong swimmer for his age and Harriet wouldn't have been able to stop him, not once he'd made up his mind. She was a law-abiding soul and only a weak swimmer anyway, so she sat and watched. We don't know for certain what happened, but it's supposed Philip got cramp. In any event, Harriet had to watch her adored brother drown.'

Philippa went cold at the thought and shivered, murmuring, 'Poor Aunt Harriet, how horrible for her!'

'It left an indelible mark on her. Somehow she felt guilty, felt she had let her parents down—which was, of course, ridiculous. Your grandparents were shattered, your grandmother was ill with grief for a long time. Harriet had help in her recovery in the form of her baby brother, your father, transferring all her passions to him.'

'Who was no substitute for his brother,' remarked Philippa with swift insight, and Francis quickly agreed.

'Robert was Philip's opposite in almost every way. He hated the mills and the weight of their inheritance hung heavy on him, even as a child. He was a popular boy, easygoing up to a point, and he did try to be what his father wanted him to be, but in the end he had to break away. Nowadays it's happening all the time, but then, for the only son to turn his back on a family business that had been going for years and years, you can imagine the outrage, can't you? Robert's going not only affected your grandparents, but Harriet as well. She had now "lost" two brothers who were her whole world. She was devastated. If she had married, things would have been different, but she stayed at home and devoted herself to her parents, and when your grandmother died, to her father.'

'And when Lucy and Ross came to Copperthwaite, she transferred some of that devotion to them,' observed Philippa pensively. 'My letter, when it arrived, posed a threat. I was the daughter of someone who had turned his back on Copperthwaite and I had no right to be part of it.' She moved restlessly, uncurled and slipped from the sofa to kneel in front of the fire. Francis watched her and sat forward, elbows on knees, his eyes never leaving her.

'I've always had a funny feeling about Harriet,' Philippa went on. 'She seemed welcoming and yet didn't do anything much to help me fit in, and I'd sometimes catch her looking at me with a peculiarly fixed expression on her face. I put it down to a slight resentment, which she had every right to feel—Ross and Lucy too—so I ignored it, hoping that as time went by they would realise I only wanted to be part of the family and hadn't come for gain.' She gave a sigh. 'Harriet would

never have believed that, would she?' She frowned
into the fire and then turned slightly to ask, 'How
did Grandfather find out about the letter?'

'Harriet confessed, the day Philip collapsed after
the party ... do you remember she had to be
sedated? She thought your grandfather was going
to die, there and then, and became emotional.
When he asked her outright if she'd destroyed
your letter all those years ago she admitted she
had—became quite hysterical.'

'It's not nice to be hated,' Philippa said
sombrely, and Francis joined her on the hearthrug
and folded his arms round her comfortingly.

'She's sick, Pippa, and needs help.' His voice
became lighter purposefully. 'Something else too.
Your grandfather periodically bought your father's
paintings, so indirectly he was responsible for your
education.'

'That's rather a nice thought.'

'Yes, isn't it? And there's a growing interest in
Robert's painting. An art dealer is interested in
putting on an exhibition of his work and I've
promised Philip to organise it, so we'll have to
look into what was packed up and sent on to you
when your father died.'

Philippa's face brightened and she turned
shining eyes to him, exclaiming, 'Now, that *is* great
news! I've always considered his work to be
undervalued.' She fell silent and after a few
moments' thought asked a little uncertainly,
'Francis, does this mean that Grandfather has
been keeping his eye on me all this time?' She
swivelled round in his arms and searched his face
intently, and Francis smiled.

'Yes, he has. First through my father, who was,
if you remember, his godson and very close, and

went frequently to Grenoble and spoke to the Head of your school, taking back reports of your wellbeing and achievements.' He paused and the smile twisted wryly. 'When my father died I took his place.'

Philippa stared at him.

He went on, 'I only went to Grenoble once, for the Leavers' Ceremony. I sat discreetly at the back of the hall and watched you walk up and receive your prizes.' He grinned. 'I have to admit that at the ripe old age of twenty-four, the eighteen-year-old Philippa Ingram was still, in my eyes, a school-kid.'

Philippa clapped a hand to her forehead and gasped, 'I can't believe it! Do you mean to say that you came . . . Oh, my goodness! It's as if a piece of a jigsaw from my life that was missing has been found, and yet I didn't know it was lost! You! No wonder you had no difficulty in recognising me at Orange.' She thought for a moment and then asked, her voice rising in wonderment, 'Francis, did you go to Oxford too?'

'I was at your graduation,' he admitted cheerfully, 'again sitting well out of the way at the back. My wretched hair doesn't help me to become part of a crowd.'

'Very difficult for you to become nondescript,' agreed Philippa teasingly, running her fingers through his mop of hair before giving an incredulous laugh. 'I still can scarcely believe all this, you know!' She smiled up into his face. 'It gives me a nice feeling to know you were there.'

'I'm glad,' replied Francis simply, and they fell silent for a moment, each thinking their own thoughts, and then Francis said pensively, 'By this time I was beginning to feel that I knew you rather well and hoped to be able to persuade Philip to get in touch with you, but he refused. He was very upset at your father's death . . .'

'I know he sent flowers,' put in Philippa. 'I had mixed feelings about that.'

'I think he was scared you'd openly show your contempt of him, a contempt which he considered was his due, but he was very proud of you, and the way you were coping with your life. He contented himself with keeping a peripheral watch on you just in case you ever needed his help.' He paused and added wryly, 'Which brings us to May of this year . . .'

'. . . and the Roman theatre at Orange,' finished Philippa slyly.

'Exactly. Philip guessed something had happened when I asked to be released from his promise not to tell you all this.' He frowned and fell silent again, continuing slowly, 'At the time, I honestly believed I went to Provence purely for Philip's sake. I know now that I must have been a little bit in love with you even then, without realising it. I had held my watching brief for ten years and was interested in meeting you. I thought I could find out your feelings on the subject of your grandfather and see if you intended to go to the party. If you were not, I was going to try and persuade you otherwise. I really did need a holiday, and Maman was making noises about not seeing me and I had some business to attend to in Europe, so when Jules told me you were visiting Sylvie it all seemed to fit together beautifully. I would go to Avignon and "accidentally" meet you, but I did more than that, didn't I? Poor fool, I came a complete cropper!' He gave a self-mocking laugh, and traced her profile lightly with a finger.

Philippa caught his hand and kissed it, saying

fiercely, 'So did I! Ah, Francis, so did I!'

'Jules watched it all happening with great delight, as you can imagine,' Francis told her drily, tucking her into the crook of his arm more comfortably. 'He did say that perhaps I should tell you of my involvement with your grandfather, but all that seemed totally unimportant. This was just me and you, and I wanted it to stay that way until I was forced to do otherwise. I realised how stupid that was when I returned earlier than I expected to the inn at La Garde-Freinet and found you gone.'

'I didn't know what to believe,' Philippa admitted softly against his chest. 'I panicked and ran away.'

'I have something for you,' said Francis, feeling in his pocket and bringing out a handkerchief which he unrolled into the palm of his hand. 'As instructed, Sylvie gave me these. Poor Sylvie! She kept saying how sorry she was, but that wasn't much consolation. She did, however, hint that you would cross by Cherbourg.'

'The wretch!' exclaimed Philippa comfortably.

'Time to put these on again, don't you think?'

'I've always wanted to be draped in diamonds and nothing but diamonds,' Philippa declared huskily, and in one fluid movement she slipped the dressing-gown from her shoulders and sat quietly while Francis fastened the necklace round her throat and slipped the wedding ring and solitaire on her finger.

With the firelight as a backcloth, he searched her face and she put her arms round his neck and whispered,

'I won't run away again, Francis, I promise,' and drew him tenderly to her.

*   *   *

Ross said, 'Hello, Philippa. I'm glad you came.'
He took her hands in his and studied her for a
moment. 'I'm only sorry your return visit is for a
sad reason.' He kissed her cheek and held out a
hand to Francis. 'Come into the library, there's a
good fire going—and we need one, don't we? The
graveside was so bleak, but at least the snow held
off for a while.' He ushered them in and closed the
door behind them, smiling at them. 'You're both
looking very well,' he went on in a lighter vein, the
smile lingering, and Francis answered,

'Thank you for keeping out of the way
yesterday, Ross.'

Ross inclined his head, accepting the thanks,
and Philippa looked from one to the other with
pretty uncertainty. 'For keeping out of the way?'
she echoed, and when Francis merely smiled
without replying, Ross explained.

'I met the train, just in case. Don't get me
wrong, Francis, I trust you implicitly, but Philippa
might not have wanted to go with you. I just
waited long enough to make sure.' He grinned, his
eyes dancing. 'There was no doubt as to the
warmth of your welcome.'

'Oh, Ross, how kind of you!' exclaimed
Philippa, giving him a hug. 'You do care what
happens to me!'

'Of course I do, stupid,' Ross asserted, going
bright red. He addressed Francis. 'I thought you'd
caught sight of me, but I was glad you
telephoned.'

Seeing Philippa's bewildered face, Francis said,
'I rang Copperthwaite to say we'd arrived home
safely, and to put Ross's mind at rest I told him
about us.'

Philippa gave Ross an apologetic grimace. 'How

I shall be glad when everyone knows. The whole thing is too embarrassing for words, and the only way to get through it is to give absolutely no explanations!'

Ross laughed and put an arm round each of them, saying, 'Congratulations, Francis, I admire your choice,' and planting a kiss on Philippa's cheek added, 'and you, cousin, keep a good secret. I'm glad all your problems have worked out.' He glanced at his watch. 'We'd better go in. Mr Harkness said three o'clock. By the way, I should warn you that Harriet is in a bad way. She's cracked completely and is insisting on being present, although the doctor says she should be in bed. He's given her something to calm her down. Unfortunately, she's taken against you, Philippa, for some reason. I hope you'll bear with her.'

'Don't worry, Ross,' soothed Philippa, and slipped her hand into Francis' for comfort.

They followed Ross into the drawing-room where Mr Harkness, the family solicitor, had set out his papers. He came forward to greet them, face and voice subdued as warranted the occasion but his eyes bright and his handshake warm.

'May I congratulate you, Francis, on your good news?' He swung round to Philippa. 'I know your grandfather was delighted, Mrs Balfour,' and he retained Philippa's hand and led her to a chair.

Philippa murmured a reply, her cheeks reddening, heard Lucy give a gasp of surprise and sought out her aunt, who was sitting in an armchair in the corner. Harriet was extremely pale and seemed to have shrunk in stature. Ross crossed to the chair and knelt down by her side, taking her hand, saying,

'Harriet—Francis and Philippa are married.

Isn't that a pleasant surprise?'

Philippa smiled at her aunt and saw a look of anger pass over the blank features, and realised that Harriet had wanted Francis for Lucy—something else for her hatred to feed on.

'Married!' exclaimed Lucy, her eyes wide. 'You secretive pair!'

Mr Harkness cleared his throat and returned to the table. 'I think we should begin, don't you? Everyone in this room is a beneficiary.' He glanced over his spectacles and allowed his gaze to cover them all. 'This is the last Will and Testament of Philip Robert Ingram, of this address, dated . . .'

Philippa listened in surprise, for the will was dated seven years previously, just after her father was killed.

It was quite simple. Bequests were made to the servants for long and faithful service. Harriet was to be allowed to live her life out at Copperthwaite, if that was her wish, and was given an annuity. The house and contents, together with shares in Copperthwaite Mills, were left to Philippa. Ross and Lucy were left sums of money and shares in the Company. The number of shares that Francis held was increased and he was named as successor to the Board of Directors.

'A fair will, in my opinion,' expounded Mr Harkness, smiling all round. 'I share the duties of Executor with Francis Balfour, and we will let you know when all the formalities have been dealt with.'

Harriet said flatly, 'Father made the will seven years ago.' Her eyes swung round wildly to Philippa. 'Before he ever met you!' Her voice rose. 'I didn't want you to come here!'

'Yes, I know, Aunt,' soothed Philippa. Harriet burst out, 'I didn't want you to come,' and pulled her handkerchief between agitated fingers.

'Miss Ingram, I think you would be better in your room, lying down quietly.' Mr Harkness approached her and encouraged her to rise from the chair and take his arm.

'I'll get some tea brought up to you. You'd like that, wouldn't you?' coaxed Ross. 'Some bread and butter, and cake too?'

'He left you Copperthwaite!' accused Harriet venomously, stopping in front of Philippa and fixing her with a wild stare. Mr Harkness and Ross urged her on, but she acquired strength and resisted them. 'Robert doesn't deserve Copperthwaite! He left it! He left me! They've all left me!' This ended on a savage cry. The passion seeped away and with a curious lack of intonation which made the words more intense, she added, 'I'm not sorry about the letter,' which sent a shiver down Philippa's spine and she clutched for Francis' hand which grasped hers tightly.

Ross said quietly, 'Come, Harriet,' and he drew her to the door where she held back, her eyes seeking out Philippa, and when she finally left, the tension eased, and everyone seemed to let out a long-held-in breath.

Mr Harkness, well used to awkward situations, declined refreshment, saying that because of the weather he felt that he should be getting home. Francis went with him to see him off and when he returned Ross had rejoined them, the tea trolley hard at his heels.

'Are we allowed an explanation now?' demanded Lucy, her eyes darting between Francis and Philippa. 'What's this letter that Harriet says she's not sorry about?'

Francis raised a brow at Philippa and she pulled

a rueful face and murmured, 'You tell,' and he then recounted the main details—that Philip Ingram had been secretly monitoring his granddaughter all her life; that Harriet had held back a letter written by Philippa to her grandfather when she was a child; that he and Philippa had met in Provence earlier in the year and had married; and finally, that Philippa had decided to come to Cumbria to meet them all and acquaint herself with the family.

'But why didn't you come together? Why pretend you didn't know each other?' asked Lucy, puzzled, and Francis replied coolly,

'Because Philippa wasn't too sure of my motives.' He sent his wife a wicked look. 'She thought I was marrying her for her money.'

'But, Philippa,' exclaimed Lucy, turning an incredulous face to her cousin, 'Francis is awfully rich!'

'Don't be vulgar,' said Ross, tweaking her hair.

Everyone laughed, and the tea was poured and plates handed round. Lucy came and sat down beside Philippa, looking at her as though properly for the first time. She said, a little abruptly,

'You won't be bothered with me around here for much longer. I'm moving to London—we're negotiating for premises and going to hit the big city with our talents.' She pulled a face. 'Ross says I haven't been very welcoming towards you.' She gave a shrug. 'I suppose I did feel a bit resentful about you coming, but without realising it I probably took my cue from Harriet. I'm sorry.'

'I understand,' Philippa replied, and Lucy gave a laugh.

'Yes, I think you do.' Her eyes went to Francis, talking to her brother. 'As much as I'm capable, I've always loved him, but he thinks it's only a hangover from a schoolgirl crush—and perhaps it is. Anyway, he's never thought of me that way.'

'Thank you for telling me.'

'Don't say anything to him, will you?'

'No, I won't,' promised Philippa, and Lucy gave a little nod, said, 'Good luck,' and wandered off. Philippa took some pains to catch Ross by himself and assured him that nothing would change at Copperthwaite.

He sighed, frowning slightly. 'We'll take each day as it comes. Lucy tells me she's off to London, while I . . .' He hesitated, and Philippa teased,

'You'll be working on your new designer, persuading her that her future lies with the Copperthwaite Mills and Ross Fairley in particular!'

Ross laughed. 'You see too much, cousin.' He tucked her hand in his arm and they walked across the hall.

'Would you consider living here, Ross?'

'No. It's your birthright, Philippa. Do you hate the place?'

'Goodness, no—I can imagine it to be a happy house, with children growing up here.' She became excited by the thought. 'We shall have holidays together here—the Morin cousins and their children and yours and Lucy's . . .'

'What are you planning now?' asked Francis, joining them and putting his arm round his wife.

'. . . and ours, of course,' went on Philippa, warming to her theme. 'Holidays to remember.'

'A little precipitate,' drawled Francis, 'but a nice idea.'

On the drive back to Inglewood, Philippa found she was turning the plain gold band on her finger, still not used to it being there.

'Peter Farnsworth told me you'd recommended me to his company,' she said.

'Peter has a large mouth,' declared Francis drily.

'Have you been putting business my way, Francis?' She stared at him and caught a too innocent look in return. 'You have! What a devious man you are!'

Francis laughed and shook his head. 'I merely put your name forward, if ever the occasion arose. If you got the job then it was purely on merit!'

Philippa smiled and made no answer. After a moment she said soberly, 'I suppose Grandfather had to leave me the house.' It was not quite a question, but Francis answered it as such.

'Of course he did. Your father would have inherited it had he been alive, and you, as his only child, were next in line. One of the reasons Philip was delighted to learn of our marriage was that there was a chance of children growing up there again.'

'I thought I was pregnant when I came back to England,' offered Philippa, in a small voice, 'but it was a false alarm.'

'Yes, I know.' Francis held his breath and then gave a soft, 'Damn!'

Philippa, dreaming about Francis's baby, blond and blue-eyed, registered what he had said and swung her head round. 'You knew?' she asked, and gave a resigned sigh. 'Grace.'

'Not her fault, Pippa darling, I swear it. I telephoned—I had to know how you were. She was very strict, we didn't talk about anything other than your health. I think I could get to like Grace—there's a no-nonsense charm about her.' He grinned. 'I tell a lie. We did, once, talk about

Beau and she waxed eloquent on the subject.'

That evening, relaxing by the fire, Francis drew a letter from his pocket, saying, 'I've heard from Jules. He and Lisette have set the date for their wedding.' He handed it to Philippa, who scanned the pages quickly, looking up with a smile to say,

'A June date. It will be lovely to spend our first anniversary over there. I must write to Sylvie and tell her everything is right between us.' She paused. 'It is, isn't it, Francis?'

'Extremely right,' he confirmed, putting a finger beneath her chin and drawing her face round to his. 'I knew you were angry and hurt by my deception, but I didn't think it was totally that which sent you running. I had to make myself have patience because I sensed you needed time to sort yourself out. Am I right?'

She nodded. 'I was all mixed up, about my identity, I suppose. And Copperthwaite and Grandfather must have been lying dormant for a long time. On an emotional level, your involvement there seemed incredibly right, but on a mental one, it appeared horribly sinister—and yet I never stopped loving you.'

'I'm very glad to hear it. Come along, I have something to show you.' Francis pulled her up from the sofa and led her through the hallway and into another room off. 'This is my study, for want of a better word,' he said, 'and I want you to see this,' and he put on a wall light and they stood looking at a picture.

It was a portrait of a young girl sitting with her arms full of poppies. Wild grasses, sprinkled with splashes of red, danced in the breeze against a backcloth of a Mediterranean blue sky.

'*Girl with Poppies,*' breathed Philippa, and

turned to Francis, her eyes wide. 'Where did you get this, Francis?'

He looked from her to the portrait and back again. 'I came across it two years ago. The supply of your father's pictures had, rather naturally, dried up, but this was unearthed in a gallery in Paris, one I frequent regularly. The owner is a friend of mine and I'd asked him if ever he came across a Robert Ingram could he put it on one side for me to look at. Where this one came from originally we don't know. He'd picked it up at a sale in Lyons.'

'You mean you've had it for two years?' Philippa gazed at the picture wonderingly and turned to find his eyes upon her, the look on his face bringing a confused warmth to her cheeks.

'So you see,' Francis said gravely, 'you've been part of me for all that time without knowing it.'

'I was about sixteen. It's good, isn't it?'

'Very good. I'll loan it to the Ingram exhibition, but it's not for sale,' claimed Francis firmly. 'I'm greedy—I want both the portrait and the original!' His lips brushed hers before he walked her to the desk at the far end of the room. 'I half-thought I'd give you the painting for a wedding present, but I found I couldn't part with my Poppy Girl, and then I had another idea. I hope you like it.' He leaned over and opened a drawer, taking out an envelope which he handed to her.

Philippa looked at the manila envelope thoughtfully and drew out the papers inside. She began to read them, registering that they were the title deeds to Poppy Cottage.

She lifted a glowing face. 'Francis, how good you are!'

'Rubbish!' The colour flooded his face.

'How did you know that I desperately wanted to rescue the cottage?'

'I just guessed.' He took back the envelope and dropped it into the drawer, then holding her close, 'We'll start putting the renovations in hand now—they have a leisurely work-pace, the French artisan! And in June, when we go for Jules' and Lisette's wedding, we'll see how things are progressing.'

Philippa smiled up at him. 'That sounds wonderful.' She tilted her head. 'There's someone else I shall visit, to pay my respects,' she said, purposely enigmatic, 'and to offer up my thanks.'

Francis eyed her for a moment and as understanding dawned he grinned and asked, 'May I come too?'

The sun was high in a blue, cloudless sky, its rays beating down on the statue of the Emperor Augustus as he stood regally in his arched niche overlooking the vast auditorium. The doors of the Roman theatre at Orange had just been re-opened after the midday break and a few tourists were coming in, forerunners of another busy afternoon in this second week of June.

A brown-eyed, long-limbed woman, glowing with good health and vitality, climbed steadily up the stone steps, taking one or two rests on the way, until she finally reached the top. She watched the fair-haired man leisurely following her, smiling down at him, and then allowed her gaze to envelop the whole theatre, finally remaining on the statue of the Emperor Augustus.

Reaching her, Francis followed the direction of her gaze and asked teasingly, 'Have you given thanks?'

Philippa threw out her arms, embracing everything before her. 'I've given thanks to whoever is out there listening,' she declared soberly, spinning round to look out over the roof-tops. 'Francis, I do believe that's the same pigeon strutting on that chimney—look, do you see him?' She gave a long, happy sigh and studied her husband thoughtfully. 'I've never asked, but did you know I'd be here, when we first met?'

Francis grinned. 'I wasn't as clever as that—no, how could I have known? That I should meet you at Sylvie's dinner party, yes, but our actual meeting was entirely accidental.'

'The gods were on our side then,' declared Philippa delightedly. 'Did you recognise me right away?'

Francis leaned back against the wall, his elbows resting on the ledge. 'Jules had mentioned you were driving a red Metro and I remembered the number. I saw it parked outside, and thought you might be in the theatre. I had genuinely gone for tickets for *The Dream*, hoping to entice you into coming with me, and I dragged Lisette inside—she thought I was crazy.'

'And I thought she was your *bonne amie*,' offered Philippa slyly.

'Good—that means you were showing some interest even then.'

She turned her head and laughed into his eyes and leaned back against him, her bare arm brushing his. 'You pack a powerful punch, *monsieur*. I couldn't understand why you should be having such an effect on me and it be so one-sided.'

'One-sided be damned!' scoffed Francis rudely. 'When you turned round and I found myself staring at the girl in my picture I was landed such a wallop, the whole place somersaulted! If I seemed cool and composed it was some good acting on my part.'

Philippa slipped her arm through his, laughter trembling her voice. 'You're just trying to get round me. I was sixteen when Dad painted that portrait, which happens to be over ten years ago.'

'You don't look more than ten days older,' declared Francis lovingly.

She glanced down at herself and then sought his eyes, her own dancing. 'There's a bit more of me.' She patted the bump under the baggy cotton dungarees she was wearing, adding softly, 'And I've offered up thanks for this too.'

Francis covered her hand with his and they both felt a kick.

'Wow—I reckon he's going to be a Rugby player!' gasped Philippa, laughing and Francis said teasingly, 'He could be a she.' He glanced at his watch. 'I think we'd better make tracks. You ought to have a rest before we go to Sylvie and Fabien's party.' They began to walk slowly down the steps, Francis giving Philippa a hand down. She gave a chuckle.

'Did you know Sylvie had Jules lined up for me?'

'The devil she had!'

'She reckons she knew that was a non-starter the minute she saw us together. You did stare rather,' and Philippa smiled complacently.

Francis stopped their descent and said softly, 'I couldn't believe you were real.'

'Excuse me, do you speak English?'

As one, they turned to the speaker. He was holding a ten-franc note.

'Oh, lord!' breathed Philippa, laughter bubbling up inside. 'This is where we came in!'

'It's for the . . .'

'Yes, yes, we know—and here,' Francis delved into his pocket, 'do have these, with our compliments.' He thrust the two coins into the surprised Englishman's hand, and with a beaming smile drew Philippa towards the exit and their laughter floated lightly in the air.

The Englishman watched them go, their laughter infectious and making him smile.

The Emperor Augustus looked on.

Janet Dailey
Americana

Don't miss a single title from this great collection. The first eight titles have already been published. Complete and mail this coupon today to order books you may have missed.

Harlequin Reader Service

In U.S.A.
901 Fuhrmann Blvd.
P.O. Box 1397
Buffalo, N.Y. 14140

In Canada
P.O. Box 2800
Postal Station A
5170 Yonge Street
Willowdale, Ont. M2N 6J3

Please send me the following titles from the Janet Dailey Americana Collection. I am enclosing a check or money order for $2.75 for each book ordered, plus 75¢ for postage and handling.

_____	ALABAMA	Dangerous Masquerade
_____	ALASKA	Northern Magic
_____	ARIZONA	Sonora Sundown
_____	ARKANSAS	Valley of the Vapours
_____	CALIFORNIA	Fire and Ice
_____	COLORADO	After the Storm
_____	CONNECTICUT	Difficult Decision
_____	DELAWARE	The Matchmakers

Number of titles checked @ $2.75 each = $_____

N.Y. RESIDENTS ADD
   APPROPRIATE SALES TAX $_____

Postage and Handling $ .75

                              TOTAL $_____

I enclose _____

(Please send check or money order. We cannot be responsible for cash sent through the mail.)

PLEASE PRINT

NAME _____

ADDRESS _____

CITY _____

STATE/PROV. _____

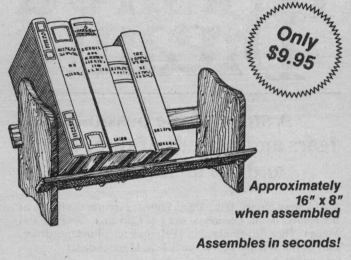

Take 4 novels and a surprise gift FREE

Here's how to get this special offer from Harlequin!

November
BETTY NEELS
TREASURY EDITION
COUPON

As simple as 1...2...3!

1. **Each month, save one Treasury Edition coupon from your favorite Romance or Presents novel.**
2. **In four months you'll have saved four Treasury Edition coupons (only one coupon per month allowed).**
3. **Then all you have to do is fill out and return the order form provided, along with the four Treasury Edition coupons required and $2.95 for postage and handling.**

Mail to: Harlequin Reader Service

In the U.S.A.	In Canada
901 Fuhrmann Blvd.	P.O. Box 609
P.O. Box 1397	Fort Erie, Ontario
Buffalo, NY 14240	L2A 9Z9

BN-Nov-2

Please send me my Special copy of the Betty Neels Treasury Edition. I have enclosed the four Treasury Edition coupons required and $2.95 for postage and handling along with this order form. (Please Print)

NAME_____

ADDRESS_____

CITY_____

STATE/PROV._____ZIP/POSTAL CODE_____

SIGNATURE_____

This offer is limited to one order per household.

This special Betty Neels offer expires
February 28, 1987.

SUPPLIES LIMITED

![Harlequin] *Harlequin Signature Edition*

Claire Harrison

ARCTIC ROSE

A small plane crashes. Two passengers survive—
Rebecca Clark and Guy McLaren. They face two
lonely months in the wilderness of Canada's
Northwest Territories.

It is a time of hardship and pain, but also
becomes a time of self-discovery and
recognition . . . a time for the celebration of life
and love.
